SARA, *and the Foreverness*

of Friends of a Feather

*An inspired narrative of a child's
experiential journey into the knowingness
that all is well. (It really is.)*

Sara receives the Award of Excellence

Body Mind Spirit Magazine, one of the widest known publishers of New Thought materials, has recently informed us that our beloved Sara has received their Award of Excellence, as one of last year's outstanding books in print. And as such, has been included as one of the forty-six books recognized in their magazine's Books to Live By selection.

Esther and I were most pleased to learn that our dear friend Louise Hay's *Hay House* publication of another dear friend, Alan Cohen's book, *A Deep Breath of Life*, has also received the recognition.

"Dear Mr. & Mrs. Hicks: It is my pleasure to inform you that Sara, and the Foreverness of Friends of a Feather has received a 1997 Body Mind Spirit Award of Excellence as one of 1996's outstanding books in print...

"Chosen from hundreds of excellent books in print in the areas of spirituality, natural healing, relationships and creativity...each book makes a valuable contribution to our self-knowledge and self-transformation...We commend the authors for their outstanding works..."

And, Esther and I feel both appreciative of and blessed by the recognition of our Sara.

TWO NEW SARA SEQUELS ARE NOW AVAILABLE:

Sara & Seth,
Solomon's Fine Featherles Friends
&
A Talking Owl Is Worth A Thousand Words

Books By Abraham-Hicks:

A New Beginning I — 1988
Handbook for Joyous Survival

A New Beginning II — 1991
A Personal Handbook to Enhance Your
Life, Liberty and Pursuit of Happiness

Sara, Book 1
The Foreverness
of Friends of A Feather — 1995
An inspired narrative of a child's
experiential journey into the knowingness
that All Is Well, (It really is.)

The Science of Deliberate Creation
Daily Planning Calendar/Workbook — 1996
A 365 Day Course in Spiritual Practicality

Sara, Book 2
Sara & Seth, Solomon's
Fine Featherless Friends — 1999
A fresh, fast paced, fun-filled adventure in wisdom.
A giant step in your journey of becoming.

Sara, Book 3
A Talking Bird
Is Worth A Thousand Words — 2002
A remarkable new way of looking
at some old ways of having fun...
An exciting adventure in joy.

If your favorite local bookstore doesn't carry these books,
they may be ordered directly or online from www.abraham-hicks.com

SARA, *and the Foreverness*

of Friends of a Feather

Esther and Jerry Hicks

Illustrated by Caroline Garrett

For information:
Jerry and Esther Hicks
P.O. Box 690070
San Antonio, TX 78269
(830) 755-2299

Illustrations Copyright © 1995 Caroline S. Garrett

Printed in the U.S.A.
First edition, April, 1995
Second printing, December, 1995
Third printing, December, 1996
Fourth printing, January 1998
Fifth printing, March, 2000
Sixth printing, February, 2002
Seventh printing, December, 2003

Library of Congress Catalog Card Number
95-94467
Hicks, Esther and Jerry
Sara, and the Foreverness of Friends of a Feather
ISBN: 0-9621219-4-0

Abraham-Hicks Publications

Foreword

Here is an inspiring as well as inspired book about a child's experiential journey into unlimited joyousness. Sara is a shy, withdrawn ten year old girl who is not very happy. She has an obnoxious brother who constantly teases her, cruel and unfeeling classmates, and an apathetic attitude towards her schoolwork. In short, she represents a lot of kids in our society today. When I first read this book, I was struck by the similarities between Sara and my ten year old. Sara is really a composite of all children.

Sara wants to feel good and happy and loving but as she looks around, she doesn't find much to feel that way about. This all changes when she meets Solomon, a wise old owl, who shows her how to see things differently through the eyes of unconditional love. He teaches Sara how to always be in an atmosphere of pure, positive energy. Sara sees for the first time who she really is and her unlimited potential. You, as the reader, will realize this is so much more than a children's story. This is a blueprint for attaining the joy and happiness that are your birthright.

My whole family read this book and we haven't been the same since. My husband, perhaps, was the most moved by it. He actually said that it had such a tremendous impact on him that he looks at life with new eyes. It's like being nearsighted your whole life and then finally getting glasses. Everything becomes crystal clear.

I cannot say enough good things about this life-transforming book. You will share in Sara's ups and downs on the way to greater heights of fulfillment and know that there is a Sara in all of us. If there is only one book you ever buy, make sure it is this one. You won't regret it! (all ages).

by Denise Tarsitano in the
"Rising Star Series

Powerful. Magical. Empowering

"*Sara*" is the heart warming novel of a girl who discovers the secrets of creating a happy life. And as Sara discovers how to create a better life for herself by starting right where she lives — the reader also learns the same lessons. Magically, both are transformed.

Reading this refreshing and inspiring new book can awaken all readers to the inner power they already have for creating the kind of life they've always wished for.

"*Sara*" is a book you will want to give to your family and friends because it conveys powerful messages about life in a manner that is easy to understand and digest.

The author's inspired writing weaves an enchanting spell that can change lives just by reading it. And while this is not specifically a "children's book", Sara *is a life transforming story for the child in each of us.*

Powerful. Magical. Empowering. "Read it."

— *Joe Vitale, author of "The Seven Lost Secrets of Success"*

This wonderful little book is a gem, elegant in its clarity of message. Its teachings fly straight to the heart, connecting to the Sara in each of us! A gentle, charming story, it is sometimes funny, often poignant, and, most of all, wonderfully joyful. It will surely become a primer for students of well-being.

— *Audrey Harbur Bershen, M.S.W., A.C.S.W.*
Psychotherapist

Preface

"People would rather be entertained than informed." That was, I believe, an observation of the eminent publisher, William Randolph Hearst. If so, then to inform in an entertaining manner would seem to be the most effective mode of conveying information, even information of great personal value.

"Sara, and the Foreverness of Friends of a Feather" both entertains and informs as it flows to you — as per your state of attraction — through the Universal thought translation process of Esther and her word processor. Streams of impeccable wisdom and unconditional love — gently taught by Sara's very entertaining feathered mentor — blend with the currents of Sara's enlightening experiences with her family, peers, neighbors and teachers to lift you to a new awareness of your natural state of well-being. Of your knowing that all is really well.

Consider who you are and why you are here as you are considering studying this book, and then, at the completion of your first leisurely reading of this book, take note of how far and how fast you have progressed toward all that is important to you.

As a result of the clearer perspectives that you will have gained from this brief, simple, thought-provoking novel, expect to experience a new level of joyous fulfillment.

Jerry & Esther Hicks

PART I

*Sara and the Foreverness of
Friends of a Feather*

CHAPTER ONE

Sara frowned as she lay in her warm bed, disappointed to find herself awake. It was still dark outside, but Sara knew it was time to get up. *I hate these short winter days,* Sara thought, *I wish I could just stay here until the sun comes up.*

Sara knew she had been dreaming. It was something very pleasant although she had no idea now what the dream had been about.

I don't want to be awake yet, Sara thought, as she tried to adjust from her pleasant dream into her not-so-pleasant cold winter morning. Sara snuggled down deep into her warm bed and listened to hear if her mother was up and moving about yet. She pulled the blankets up over her head, and closed her eyes and tried to recall a piece of the very pleasant dream she had awakened from. It had been so delicious, Sara wanted more.

Darn. I really need to use the bathroom. I'll just hold still and relax and maybe I won't notice.

Sara shifted her position, trying to delay the inevitable. *It's not working. Okay. I'm up. Another day. Big deal.*

Sara tiptoed down the hall into the bathroom, carefully stepping over the spot in the floor that always creaked, and quietly closed the door. She decided to put off flushing the toilet so that she could enjoy the luxury of actually being awake and alone. *Just five more minutes of peace and quiet,* Sara thought.

"Sara? Are you up? Come here and help me!"

"Might as well flush the toilet," Sara muttered. "Okay, I'll be right there!" she called to her mother.

She could never figure out how her mother always seemed to know what everyone in the house was doing. *She must have bugging devices hidden in every room,* Sara bitterly decided. She knew that was not really true, but her negative mental rampage was well under way, and it seemed that there was no stopping it.

I'm going to stop drinking anything before I go to bed. Better yet, from noon on, I won't drink anything. Then, when I wake up, I can just lie in bed and think, all to myself — and no one will know I'm awake.

I wonder how old you are when you stop enjoying your own thoughts? I know that it happens, because no one else is ever quiet.

They can't be listening to their own thoughts, 'cause they're always talking, or watching television, and when they get in the car, the first thing they do is turn the radio on. Nobody seems to like to be alone. They always want to be with somebody else. They want to go to a meeting or to a movie or to a dance or to a ball game. I'd like to put a blanket of quiet over everything so I could, just for a little while, hear myself think. I wonder if it's possible to be awake and not be bombarded with other people's noise.

I'm going to organize a club. People against OPN. Member requirements include: You can like others, but you do not need to talk to them. You can like watching others, but do not need to explain to anybody else what you saw. You have to like to be alone, sometimes, to just think your own thoughts. It's okay to want to help others, but you must be willing to keep that to a minimum, because that's a trap that will ruin you for sure. If you are too helpful, it's all over. They'll consume you with their ideas, and you won't have any time for yourself. You must be willing to lay low and watch others without them being aware of you.

I wonder if anybody else would like to join my club. No, that would ruin it! My club is about not needing clubs! It's about my life being important enough, interesting enough, fun enough, that I don't need anybody else.

"Sara!"

Startled, Sara blinked as she came back into awareness that she was standing in front of the bathroom sink, blankly staring into the mirror, with her toothbrush half-heartedly moving around in her mouth.

"Are you going to stay in there all day? Let's get moving. We have lots to do!"

CHAPTER TWO

"Sara, did you have something you wanted to say?"

Sara jumped, becoming aware again as Mr. Jorgensen said her name.

"Yes, sir. I mean, about what, sir?" Sara stammered while the other 27 students in her classroom snickered.

Sara had never understood why they took such delight in someone else's embarrassment, but they never failed to do just that, laughing, raucously, as if something actually funny had happened. *What is funny about someone else feeling bad?* Sara just couldn't sort out the answer to that, but now wasn't the time to ponder that, anyway, for Mr. Jorgensen was still holding her in the unbelievable spotlight of discomfort while her classmates looked on with exaggerated glee.

"Can you answer the question, Sara?"

More laughing. *Would this never end.*

"Stand up, Sara, and give us your answer."

Why is he being so mean? Is this really so important?

Five or six eager hands shot up around the classroom, as show-off classmates took further delight in making Sara look bad.

"No, sir." Sara whispered, slipping down into her seat.

"What did you say, Sara?" the teacher barked.

"I said, no, sir, I do not know the answer to the question," Sara said, a bit louder. But Mr. Jorgensen was not finished with Sara, not yet.

"Do you know the question, Sara?"

Sara's face flushed red with embarrassment. She did not have the slightest idea what the question was. She had been deep in her own thoughts, truly in her own world.

"Sara, may I offer a suggestion to you?"

Sara did not look up, because she knew that giving her permission or not giving it would not stop Mr. Jorgensen.

"I suggest, young lady, that you spend more time thinking about the important things that are discussed here in this classroom, and less time gazing out of the window, wasting your time on idle, needless thoughts. Try to put something in that empty head of yours." More laughter.

Will this class never end?

And then the bell, finally the bell.

Sara walked slowly home, watching her red boots sinking into the white snow. Grateful for the snowfall. Grateful for the quiet. Grateful for an opportunity to retreat into the privacy of her own mind as she began her two mile walk home.

She noticed that the water beneath the Main Street Bridge was nearly completely covered with ice, and she thought about sliding down the river bank to see how thick the ice was, but decided to do that on another day. She was able to see the water flowing beneath the ice, and she smiled as she pondered how many different faces this river showed throughout the year. This bridge, crossing this river, was her favorite part of her walk home. There was always something interesting happening here.

Once across the bridge, Sara looked up for the first time since leaving the school yard, and she felt a little twinge of sadness wash over her as she realized that her quiet walk in solitude was only two blocks from ending. She slowed her pace to savor the peace she had rediscovered, and then turned and walked backwards for a bit, looking back at the bridge.

"Oh well," she sighed, softly, as she entered the graveled driveway to her house. She paused on the steps to kick at a large sheet of ice, loosening it with her boot and kicking it off into a snow bank. Then she pulled off her wet boots and went into the house.

Quietly closing the door, and hanging her heavy wet coat on the hook, Sara made as little noise as possible. She was not at all like the other members of her family who usually called out a loud, penetrating, "I'm home!" upon entering. *I'd like to be a hermit,* she concluded, walking through the living room into the kitchen. *A quiet, happy hermit, thinking, talking or not talking, getting to choose everything about my day. Yes!*

CHAPTER THREE

Her only awareness — as she lay sprawled in front of her school locker on the mud-streaked floor — was that her elbow was hurting, really hurting.

Falling down is always such a shock. It happens so fast. One moment you are upright, moving quickly forward with some very deliberate intention of being in your scat when the final bell rings, and the next minute you are lying flat on your back, immobilized, stunned, and hurting. And the worst thing in the whole world is to fall down at school, where everybody can see you.

Sara looked up into a sea of gleeful-looking faces which were grinning, snickering, or laughing right out loud. *They act like nothing like this has ever happened to them.*

Once they figured out that there was nothing as exciting as a broken bone or bleeding flesh, or a victim writhing in pain, the crowd dissolved and her ghoulish schoolmates went on with their own lives, making their way back to their classrooms.

A blue sweatered arm reached down, and a hand took hers, pulling her into a sitting position, and a girl's voice said, "Are you okay? Do you want to stand up?"

No, Sara thought, *I want to disappear,* but since that was not likely, and since the crowd had already pretty much dissolved, Sara smiled weakly, and Ellen helped her to her feet.

Sara had never spoken with Ellen before, but she had seen her in the hallways. Ellen was two grades ahead of Sara, and she had only been at Sara's school for about a year.

Sara really did not know much about Ellen, but then that was not unusual. Older kids never interacted with younger kids. There was some kind of unwritten code against that. But Ellen always smiled easily, and even though she didn't seem to have many friends, and moved about pretty much by herself, Ellen seemed perfectly happy. That may have been why Sara had noticed Ellen. Sara was a loner, too. She preferred it that way.

"These floors get so slippery when it's wet outside," Ellen said, "I'm surprised more people don't fall down in here."

Still a bit dazed, and embarrassed into numbness, Sara was not consciously focused on the words Ellen was speaking, but something about Ellen's offering was making Sara feel much better.

It was a little unsettling to Sara to find herself so affected by another person. It was truly a rare occasion for Sara to prefer the words spoken from another to the quiet retreat into her own private thoughts. This felt weird.

"Thank you," Sara murmured, as she tried to brush some of the mud from her soiled skirt.

"I don't think it will look so bad once it dries a bit," Ellen said.

And, again, it was not the words that Ellen spoke. They were just normal, everyday words, but it was something else. Something about the way she spoke them.

Ellen's calm, clear voice seemed to soothe the sense of tragedy and trauma Sara had been feeling, and Sara's enormous embarrassment all but vanished, leaving Sara feeling stronger and better.

"Oh, it doesn't really matter." Sara replied. "We'd better hurry or we'll be late."

And as she took her seat — elbow throbbing, clothes muddied, shoelaces untied, and her stringy brown hair hanging in her eyes — she felt better than she had ever felt sitting in this seat. It was not logical, but it was true.

Sara's walk home from school was different that day. Instead of withdrawing into her own quiet thoughts, noticing not much more than the narrow path in the snow before her, Sara felt alert and alive. She felt like singing. So she did. Humming a familiar tune, she moved happily down her path, watching others on their way about the small town.

As she passed the town's only restaurant, Sara considered stopping in for an after-school snack. Often, a glazed donut or an ice cream cone, or a small basket of French-fried potatoes, was just the thing to temporarily distract Sara from the long, weary day she had spent in school.

I still have all of this week's allowance, Sara thought, standing on the sidewalk in front of the small cafe, considering. But she decided not to, as she remembered her mother's often-offered words, "Don't spoil your dinner."

Sara had never understood those words because she was always ready to eat if what was offered was good. It was only when dinner didn't look good, or, more importantly, when it didn't smell good, that she found excuses to pass it by, or at least eat it sparingly. *Seems to me like somebody else is the one that spoils it,* Sara grinned to herself as she continued walking home. She really didn't need anything today, anyway — for today, all was really rather well in Sara's world.

CHAPTER FOUR

Sara stopped atop the Main Street Bridge, looking below at the ice to see if it looked thick enough to walk across. She spotted a few birds standing on the ice and noticed some rather large dog tracks in the snow on the ice, but she did not think the ice was quite yet ready for all of her weight, including her heavy coat, boots and a rather hefty bag of books. *Better wait a bit,* Sara thought, as she peered down the icy river.

Leaning way out over the ice, supported by the rusty railing, that Sara believed was there just for her own personal pleasure, and feeling better than she had felt in a long time, she decided to stay for a while to look at her wonderful river. She dropped her book bag to her feet, and leaned against her rusty metal railing, Sara's favorite place in the whole world.

Resting and leaning and appreciating this spot, Sara smiled as she remembered the day this old railing was transformed into this perfect leaning perch by Mr. Jackson's hay truck when he slammed on his brakes on the wet, icy road to avoid running over Harvey, Mrs. Peterson's dachshund. Everyone in town talked on and on, for months, about how lucky he was that his truck didn't go right into the river. Sara was always surprised at how people were always making things seem bigger and worse than they really were. If Mr. Jackson's truck had gone into the river, well, that would be quite different. That would justify the big fuss everyone made. Or if he had gone into the river and had drowned, that would have been even more reason to talk. But he didn't go into the river. As far as Sara could figure out, no harm had come from it at all. His truck was not damaged. Mr. Jackson was not damaged. Harvey was frightened and stayed home for several days, but he was not hurt in any way. *People just like to worry,* Sara concluded. But Sara was elated when she discovered her new leaning perch. Large, heavy-gauge steel posts were now bending way out over the water. So perfect, it was as if it was made especially to please and delight Sara.

Leaning out over the river, and looking downstream, Sara could see the great log stretched across the river, and that made her smile, too. That was another "accident" that suited Sara just fine.

One of the big trees that lined the river bank was badly damaged in a wind storm. So the farmer who owned the land gathered some volunteers from around town and they trimmed all of the branches from the tree, getting ready to cut it down. Sara wasn't sure why there was so much excitement about it. It was just one big, old tree.

Her father wouldn't let her get close enough to hear much of what they were saying, but Sara heard someone say that they were worried that the power lines might be too close. But then, the big saws started buzzing again, and Sara couldn't hear anything else, so she stood back at a distance, with most everyone else in town, to watch the big event.

Suddenly, the saws were quiet and Sara heard someone shout, "Oh, NO!" Sara remembered covering her ears and squeezing her eyes closed tight. It felt like the whole town shook when the huge tree fell, but when Sara opened her eyes, she squealed with delight as she got her first glimpse of her perfect log bridge connecting the little dirt paths on each side of the river.

As Sara basked in her metal nest, hanging right out over the river, she breathed deeply, wanting to take in that great river smell. It was hypnotic. The fragrances, the constant, steady sound of the water. *I love this old river,* Sara thought, still gazing at her big log, that was crossing the water downstream.

Sara loved to put her hands out for balance and see how quickly she could scoot across the log. She was never frightened, but she was always mindful that the slightest slip could take her tumbling into the river. And Sara never crossed the log that she did not hear her mother's cautious, uncomfortable words playing in her mind. "Sara, stay away from that river! You could drown!"

But Sara did not pay much attention to those words, not anymore, anyway, because she knew something that her mother did not know. Sara knew that she could not drown.

Relaxed, and at one with the world, Sara lay in her perch and remembered what had happened on that very log just two summers earlier. It had been late in the afternoon, and all of Sara's chores were done, and so, Sara had gone down to the river. She had leaned in her metal perch for a while, and then she had followed the dirt path down to the log. The river, swollen from the run-off from the melting snow, was higher than usual, and water was actually lapping up over the log. She had debated whether it was a good idea to cross over. But then, with a strange sort of whimsical enthusiasm, she decided to cross her precarious log bridge. As she got near the middle, she paused for a moment and turned sideways on the log with both feet pointing downstream, teetering back and forth only slightly, as she regained her balance and her courage. And then, from out of nowhere, came the Pittsfield's mangy mutt, Fuzzy, bounding across the bridge, happily acknowledging Sara, and bumping up against her with sufficient force to topple Sara into the very fast moving river.

Well, this is it, Sara had thought. *Just as my mother warned, I am going to drown!* But things were moving too fast for Sara to give too much thought to that. For Sara found herself on an amazing and wonderful ride as she floated rapidly downstream on her back with eyes looking upward seeing one of the most beautiful views she had ever witnessed.

She had walked these river banks hundreds of times, but this was a point of view very different from what she had noticed before. Gently carried on this amazing cushion of water, she could see blue sky up above, framed by perfectly shaped trees, denser and sparser, thicker and thinner. So many beautiful shades of green.

Sara was not aware that the water was extremely cold, but instead, she felt as if she were floating on a magic carpet, smoothly and quietly and safely.

For a moment, it seemed to be getting darker. As Sara floated into a thick grove of trees which lined the river-bank, she could see almost no sky at all.

"Wow, these trees are beautiful!" Sara said right out loud. She had never walked this far downstream. The trees were lush and lovely, and some of their limbs were dipping right down into the river.

And then, a long, friendly, solid limb seemed to reach right down into the water to give Sara a hand up.

"Thank you, tree," Sara said sweetly, pulling herself out of the river. "That was very nice of you."

She stood on the river bank, dazed but exhilarated, and tried to get her bearings.

Wow! Sara murmured as she spotted the Peterson's big red barn. She could barely believe her eyes. In what had seemed to Sara like only a minute or two, she had floated over five miles through pastures and farmland. But Sara did not mind this long walk home one bit. With delicious enthusiasm for life, Sara walked and skipped her way home.

As soon as she could get out of them, she put her dirty, wet clothes in the washing machine, and hurriedly ran a nice warm bath. *No point in giving Mother one more thing to worry about,* she had thought. *This won't make her feel safer.*

Sara lay back in the warm water, smiling, as all sorts of leaves and dirt and river bugs washed out of her curly, brown hair, knowing, with certainty, that her mother was wrong.

Sara knew that she would never drown.

CHAPTER FIVE

"Sara, wait up!" Sara stopped in the center of the intersection and waited as her little brother ran at his very top speed toward her.

"Ya gotta come, Sara, it's real neat!"

I'll bet it is, Sara thought, pondering the last several "real neat" things Jason had sprung on her. There was the barn rat Jason had trapped in his own self-made trap, that "really was alive last time I looked," Jason had promised. Twice, Jason had caught Sara off guard and had tricked her into peering into his school bag, only to find some innocent little bird, or mouse, that had fallen prey to Jason and his grungy little friends, excited and eager to use their new Christmas BB guns.

What is it with boys? Sara pondered, waiting, as Jason, tired, had now slowed to a walk, seeing that Sara was actually waiting for him. *How can they actually take pleasure in hurting poor defenseless little animals? I'd like to catch them in a trap and see how they like it,* Sara thought. *I remember when his pranks were less gory and even funny, sometimes, but Jason just seems to get meaner and meaner.*

Sara stood in the middle of the quiet country road waiting for Jason to catch up to her. She suppressed a smile as she remembered the clever hoax Jason had carried out by laying his head down on his desk, hiding his shiny rubber vomit, and then looking up with his big brown eyes, exposing his sickening prize when his teacher stood over him. Mrs. Johnson had rushed out of the room to get the janitor to deal with the mess, but when she came back, Jason announced that he had taken care of it, and Mrs. Johnson was so relieved that she didn't even ask any questions. Jason was excused to go home.

Sara was stunned at how gullible Mrs. Johnson had been, not even wondering how this vomit, which appeared fresh and runny, managed to stand in such a neat little puddle on a desk with a fairly significant slope. But then, Mrs. Johnson had not yet had as much experience with Jason as Sara had had, and, Sara admitted, he got to her more than once, in her more naive days, but no more. Sara was on to Jason.

"Sara!" Jason shouted, winded and excited.

Sara stepped back, "Jason, you don't have to yell, I'm only two feet away from you."

"Sorry." Jason gulped as he tried to catch his breath. "You gotta come! Solomon's back!"

"Who's Solomon?" Sara questioned, regretting her question as soon as it was blurted; she was not wanting to show one bit of interest in whatever Jason was babbling about.

"Solomon! You know, *Solomon.* The giant bird on Thacker's Trail!"

"I never heard of a giant bird on Thacker's Trail," Sara offered, mustering as much of a sound of boredom as she could on such short notice. "Jason, I'm not interested in any more of your stupid birds."

"This bird isn't stupid, Sara, it's gigantic! You should see it. Billy said it is bigger than his father's car. Sara, you have to come, p l e a s e."

"Jason, a bird cannot be bigger than a car."

"Yes, it can! You can ask Billy's dad! He was driving home one day and he said he saw a shadow so big he thought it was an airplane passing over him. It covered the whole car. But it wasn't an airplane, Sara, it was Solomon!"

Sara had to admit that Jason's enthusiasm for Solomon was getting to her a bit.

"I'll go some other time, Jason. I have to get home."

"Oh, Sara, please come! Solomon might not be here again. You have to come, Sara, you have to!"

Jason's persistence was beginning to worry Sara. He was not usually so intense. Ordinarily, when he felt Sara's strong will kicking in, he'd just give up and lay low and wait for another opportunity to catch her more off guard. He had learned, from much experience, that the more he pressed Sara to do something that she didn't want to do, the more impossible Sara became. But there was something different here. Jason seemed compelled in a way that Sara had not seen before, and so, to Jason's tremendous surprise and delight, Sara gave in.

"Oh, all right, Jason. Where is this giant bird?"

"His name is Solomon."

"How do you know his name?"

"Billy's dad named him. He says he's an owl. And owls are wise. So his name should be Solomon."

Sara picked up her pace to try to keep up with Jason. *He's really excited about this bird,* Sara thought. *This is weird.*

"He's in here, somewhere," Jason said. "He lives in here."

Sara was often amused at Jason's assumed confidence, when Sara knew that he knew that he really didn't know what he was talking about. But, more often than not, Sara would play along, pretending that she didn't notice. It was easier that way.

They looked into the sparsely leafed thicket, now covered with snow. They walked along a badly decaying fence row, following a narrow path in the snow, carved out by a lone dog that had apparently run along not long before them....

Sara almost never walked this path in the winter. It was out of the way of her usual walk between school and home. This was, however, a place where Sara had spent countless blissful summer hours. Sara walked along, noting all the familiar nooks and crannies, feeling good about revisiting her old path. *Best thing about this path,* Sara thought, *is that I had it mostly to myself. No cars passing, no neighbors. This is a quiet path. I should walk here more often.*

"Solomon!" Jason's voice rang out, startling Sara. She hadn't expected him to shout, so.

"Jason, don't yell at Solomon. If he is in here he won't be, if you keep that up."

"He is in here, Sara. I told you, he lives in here. And if he woulda left, we woulda seen him. He's really big, Sara, really!"

Sara and Jason walked deeper and deeper into the thicket, ducking under a rusty wire, which was one of the last remnants of this rickety old fence. They walked along slowly, feeling their way carefully, not certain what might be buried in this knee-deep snow.

"Jason, I'm getting cold."

"Just a little more, Sara. Please?"

It was more from her own curiosity than from Jason's prodding, but Sara agreed. "Okay, Jason, five more MINUTES," Sara shrieked as she stepped, waist-high, into an irrigation ditch camouflaged by the snow. The cold, wet snow came right up under Sara's coat and blouse and touched right up against her bare skin. "Okay, Jason, that's it! I'm going home!"

Jason was disappointed that they did not find Solomon, but Sara's irritation had distracted him from that. There was not much that pleased Jason more than Sara's irritation.

Jason laughed heartily as Sara shook the cold wet snow out from under her clothing.

"Oh, you think that's funny, don't you, Jason? You probably made this whole Solomon thing up just to get me wet and mad!"

Jason laughed as he ran out ahead of Sara. As much as he enjoyed her irritation, he had wisely learned to keep a safe distance. "No, Sara, Solomon is real. You'll see."

"Yea, right!" Sara quipped back at Jason.

But for some reason, Sara knew that Jason was right.

CHAPTER SIX

Sara could not remember a time that it was easy for her to concentrate on what was going on in the classroom. *School is truly the most boring place on earth,* she had concluded long ago. But this day, without exception, was the hardest day Sara had ever experienced. She could not keep her mind on what the teacher was saying. Her mind kept drifting back to the thicket. And as soon as the last bell rang, Sara stuffed her book bag into her locker and went directly there.

"I'm probably crazy," Sara murmured to herself, as she walked deeper and deeper into the thicket, making her own trail in the deep snow as she moved along. "I'm looking for a silly bird that's probably not even real. Well, if I don't see him, right away, I'm leaving. I don't want Jason to know that I'm here, or that I am even interested in this bird."

Sara stopped to listen. It was so still that she could hear her own breathing. She could not see one other living creature. Not a bird, not a squirrel. Nothing. In fact, if it were not for the tracks that Sara and Jason and the lone dog had left there, yesterday, Sara might have thought she was, indeed, the only one alive on the planet.

This was truly a beautiful winter day. The sun had been shining, brightly, all afternoon, and the top crust of the snow was shiny and wet as it was slowly melting. Everything was glistening. Ordinarily, a day like this would make Sara's heart sing. What could be better than to be off, all alone, thinking her own thoughts on a beautiful day like this? But Sara felt irritated. She had hoped that Solomon would be easy to find. Somehow, thinking about the thicket and the possibility of spotting this mysterious bird had piqued Sara's interest, but now, standing here, alone, knee-deep in snow, Sara began to feel foolish. "Where is this bird? Oh, forget it! I'm going home!"

In her frustration, Sara stood in the middle of the thicket, feeling angry and overwhelmed and somewhat confused. She started backtracking out of the thicket, the way she had come in, but then, stopped to consider if it would be faster to cross through the pasture that she so often used as a short cut during the summer months. *I'm sure the river is frozen over by now. Maybe I can cross it here somewhere where it's narrow.* Sara thought, as she ducked under the single wire fence.

Sara was surprised at how disoriented she was here in the winter. She had passed through this pasture hundreds of times. This was the pasture where her uncle kept his horse during the summer months. But everything looked very different with all of her familiar landmarks buried beneath the snow. The river was completely iced over, here, and was covered by several inches of snow. Sara stopped, trying to remember where the narrowest point was. And then, she felt the ice giving way beneath her feet — and before she knew it, she was flat on her back on the very tentative ice with cold water quickly soaking through her clothes. Sara flashed back to the amazing ride this river had given her before, and, for a moment, she felt real panic, imagining a repeat of that ride, but, in this freezing cold water, being carried downstream to a frozen death.

Have you forgotten that you cannot drown? A kind voice spoke from somewhere over Sara's head.

"Who's there?" Sara asked, looking all around, staring up into the bare trees, squinting from the glare of the sun that was glistening and reflecting off of the snow-covered everything around her. *Whoever you are, why don't you help me out of here?* Sara thought, as she lay on the cracking ice, frightened that any movement might cause the ice to give way beneath her.

The ice will hold you. Just roll over onto your knees, and crawl over here, her mysterious friend said.

So, without looking up, Sara rolled over onto her stomach, and ever so slowly she pulled herself up onto her knees.

And then, gingerly, she began crawling in the direction of the voice.

Sara was in no mood for conversation. Not now. She was wet, and very cold, and really mad at herself for doing something so stupid. What she was most interested in, right now, was getting home and changed before anyone else came home and caught her in her telltale clothes.

"I've gotta go," Sara said, squinting into the sun in the direction of whomever she had been talking to.

She began picking her way back through her own tracks, very cold and irritated by her decision to try to cross the silly river. And then it hit her, "Hey, how'd *you* know that I can never drown?" No answer came back to her.

"Where'd you go? Hey, where are you?" Sara called.

And then, the biggest bird Sara had ever seen took flight from the tree top, soared high into the sky, circled the thicket and pastures below, and disappeared into the sun.

Sara stood in amazement, squinting into the sunlight. *Solomon.*

CHAPTER SEVEN

Sara awakened the next morning, and, as usual, ducked back under the covers, bracing against beginning another day. Then she remembered Solomon.

Solomon, Sara thought, *did I really see you, or did I dream you?*

But then, as Sara became more awake she remembered going to the thicket, after school, to look for Solomon, and the ice giving way beneath her feet. *No, Solomon, you were not a dream. Jason was right. You are real.*

Sara flinched as she thought of Jason and Billy shouting their way through the thicket looking for Solomon. And then, that heavy flustered feeling that Sara always got when she thought of Jason blasting into her life, swept over her.

I won't tell Jason, or anyone, that I've seen Solomon. This is my secret.

Sara literally struggled all day long to give her attention to her teacher. Her mind kept pulling back to the glistening thicket and this gigantic, magical bird. *Did Solomon actually speak to me?* Sara pondered. *Or did I only imagine it? Maybe I was dazed from falling. Maybe I was unconscious and dreamed it. Or did it really happen?*

Sara could hardly wait to go to the thicket, again, to find out if Solomon was really real.

When the last bell rang, Sara stopped by her locker to deposit her books and then stuffed her book bag in on top of them. This may have been the second day, ever, that Sara did not lug home all of her books. She had discovered that an armload of books seemed to protect her from any intrusive classmates. They somehow provided a barrier that kept frivolous, playful intruders out of her way. But today, Sara did not want anything to slow her down. She shot out of the front doors like a bullet, heading straight for Thacker's Trail.

As Sara left the paved street and started down Thacker's Trail, she saw a very large owl sitting in plain view on a fence post right out in the open. It almost seemed as if he were waiting for her. Sara was surprised to find Solomon so easily. She had spent so much time searching for this illusive mystery bird, and now, here he was, just sitting there as if he'd always been right there.

Sara did not know quite how to approach Solomon.

What should I do? Sara thought. *It seems odd to just walk up to a big owl and say,* 'Hello, how are you today?'

Hello, how are you today? the big owl said to Sara.

Sara jumped back about a foot. Solomon laughed heartily. *I didn't mean to startle you, Sara. How are you today?*

"I'm fine, thank you. I'm just not used to talking to owls, that's all."

Oh, that's too bad. Solomon said. *Some of my very best friends are owls.*

Sara laughed. "Solomon, you're funny."

Solomon, hmmmm, the owl said. *Solomon is a nice name. Yes, I think I like it.*

Sara blushed with embarrassment. She had forgotten that they had never really been introduced. Jason had told Sara the owl was named Solomon. But Billy's father had chosen that name. "Oh, I'm very sorry," Sara said. "I should have asked you your name."

Well, I've never actually thought about that, the owl said. *Solomon is a nice name however. I do like that.*

"What do you mean, you've never thought about it. You mean, you don't have a name?"

No, not really, the owl replied.

Sara could not believe her ears. "How can you not have a name?"

Well, you see, Sara, only people need labels to identify things. The rest of us just seem to know who we are, and the labels are not that important to us. But I do like the name, Solomon. And, since you are accustomed to calling others by name, that one will do nicely for me. Yes, I do like that name. Solomon, it is.

Solomon seemed so pleased with his new name that Sara's embarrassment went away. Name or no name, this bird was certainly pleasant to talk with.

"Solomon, do you think I should tell anybody about you?"

Perhaps. In time.

"But you think I should keep you a secret, for now, right?"

That's best for a while. Until you figure out what you would say.

"Oh, yea, I guess I would sound pretty silly. 'I've got this owl friend that talks to me without moving his lips.'"

And I might <u>wisely</u> point out to you, Sara, that owls do not have lips.

Sara laughed. This was a very funny bird. "Oh Solomon, you know what I mean. How do you talk with out using your mouth? And how come I've never heard any-body else around here talking about talking to you?"

No one else around here has ever heard me. It's not the sound of my voice you are hearing, Sara. **You are receiving my thoughts.**

"I don't understand. I can hear you!"

Well, it seems like you are hearing me, and, truly, you are, but not with your ears. Not in the way you hear some other things.

Sara pulled her scarf up around her neck and pulled her stocking cap down over her ears, as a blast of cold wind swept around her.

It will be dark soon, Sara. We can visit more tomorrow. Think about what we talked about. While you are dreaming tonight, notice that you can see. Even though your eyes will be closed tight, you will see in your dreams. So, if you do not need your eyes to see, you also do not need your ears to hear.

Before Sara could point out that dreams are different from real life, Solomon said, *Good-bye Sara. Isn't this a love-ly day?* And with that, Solomon leaped into the air, and pulling with his powerful wings, he rose high above the thicket and his fence post and his tiny friend below.

Solomon, Sara thought, *you are gigantic!*

Sara remembered Jason's words, "He's gigantic, Sara, you have to come and see him!" As she made her way home through the snow, she remembered how he nearly dragged Sara to the thicket, literally running with excitement, making it hard for Sara to keep up with him. *Strange,* Sara pondered, *he was so intense about me seeing this gigantic bird, and now, in three days, he has not said one word about it. I'm surprised that he and Billy have not been out here every single day looking for Solomon. It's as though he has forgotten all about it. I'll have to remember to ask Solomon about that, tomorrow.*

Over the next days, Sara often found herself saying, "I'll have to ask Solomon about that." In fact, she had started to carry a little notebook in her pocket so she could make notes about the subjects she wanted to discuss.

It seemed there was never enough time to talk to Solomon about all the things she wanted to talk to him about. The narrow window of time between school ending and Sara needing to be home, to complete her after-school chores before her mother came home from work, was little more than thirty minutes.

It's not fair, Sara had begun to think. *I spend all day with boring teachers, not one tenth as smart as Solomon, and a measly half hour with the smartest teacher I've ever had. Hmmm, teacher. I have an owl for a teacher.* That made Sara laugh right out loud.

"I'll have to ask Solomon about that."

CHAPTER EIGHT

"Solomon, are you a teacher?"

Yes, indeed, Sara.

"But you don't talk about things that 'real' teachers, excuse me, 'other' teachers talk about. I mean, you talk about things that I'm interested in. You talk about neat stuff."

Actually, Sara, I talk only about that which you talk about. Only when you ask a question is the information that I might offer of any value to you. All of those answers that are offered without a question having been asked are truly a waste of everyone's time. Neither student nor teacher has much fun in that.

Sara thought about what Solomon had said, and she realized that unless Sara asked about it, Solomon didn't talk much about anything. "But wait, Solomon. I remember something you said without my asking a question."

And what was that, Sara?

"You said, 'Have you forgotten that you cannot drown?' The very first thing you said to me, Solomon. I didn't say a word to you. I was lying there on the ice, but I was not asking you a question."

Ah, it seems that Solomon is not the only one around here who can talk without moving his lips.

"What do you mean?"

You were asking, Sara, but not with words. Questions are not always asked with words.

"That's weird, Solomon. How can you ask something if you're not talking?"

By thinking your question. Many beings and creatures communicate through thought. In fact, more communicate that way than with words. People are the only ones who use words. But even they do much more of their communicating with thoughts than with words. Think about it.

You see, Sara, I am a wiiiiiiiise old teacher whoooooo learned long ago that giving a student information that he is not asking for is a waste of time.

Sara laughed at Solomon's corny emphasis on *w i s e* and his owl-like exaggerated *whooooo*. *I love this crazy bird,* Sara thought.

I love you too, Sara, Solomon replied.

Sara blushed, having forgotten, already, that Solomon could hear her thoughts.

And then, with no further words, Solomon lifted powerfully into the sky and was gone from Sara's view.

CHAPTER NINE

"I wish I could fly, like you, Solomon."

Why, Sara? Why would you like to fly?

"Oh, Solomon, it is so boring to have to walk around down here on the ground all the time. It's so slow. It just takes forever to get places, and you can't see much, either. Only stuff that's down here on the ground with you. Boring stuff."

Well, Sara, it seems like you haven't really answered my question.

"Yes, I did, Solomon. I said I want to fly because..."

Because you don't like to walk around down here on the boring ground. You see, Sara, you didn't tell me why you want to fly. You told me why you don't want not to fly.

"There's a difference?"

Oh yes, Sara. A big difference. Try again.

A little surprised at Solomon's new decision to nit pick, Sara began again. "Okay. I want to fly because walking isn't much fun and it takes so long to walk around down here on the ground."

Sara, can you see that you are still talking more about what you don't want and why you don't want it? Try again.

"Okay. I want to fly because... I don't get this, Solomon. What do you want me to say?"

I want you to talk about what you do *want, Sara.*

"I WANT TO FLY!" Sara shouted, feeling annoyed at Solomon's inability to understand her.

Now, Sara, tell me why you want to fly. What would that be like? How would it feel? Make it feel real to me, Sara. Describe to me, what does flying feel like? I don't want you to tell me what it's like down on the ground, or what it is like NOT to fly. I want you to tell me what it is like to fly.

Sara closed her eyes, now catching the spirit of what Solomon was getting at, and began to speak. "Flying feels very free, Solomon. It's like floating, but faster."

Tell me, what you would see if you were flying?

"I would see the whole town down below. I would see Main Street and cars moving and people walking. I would see the river. I would see my school."

How does flying feel, Sara? Describe what it feels like to fly.

Sara paused with her eyes closed and pretended that she was flying high above her town. "It would be so much fun, Solomon! Flying just has to be so much fun. I could soar fast as the wind. It would feel so free. It feels so good,

Solomon!" Sara continued, now completely absorbed in her imagined vision. And then, suddenly, with the same sense of power that Sara had felt in Solomon's wings as she had seen him lift off his post day after day, Sara felt a whoosh within her that took her breath away. Her body felt, for a moment, as if it weighed ten thousand pounds, and then, instantly, she felt absolutely weightless. And then, Sara was flying.

"Solomon," Sara squealed with delight, "look at me, I'm flying!"

Solomon was flying right along with her, and together they soared high above Sara's town. The town where Sara was born. The town that Sara had walked nearly every square inch. The town that Sara was now discovering from a vantage point she had never dreamed possible.

"Wow! Solomon, this is great! Oh, Solomon, I love this!"

Solomon smiled and enjoyed Sara's extraordinary enthusiasm.

"Where are we going, Solomon?"

You may go wherever you would like to go.

"Oh, wow!" Sara blurted, looking down at her quiet little town. It had never before looked so beautiful.

Sara had seen her town from the air once before when her uncle had taken Sara and her family up in his small airplane. But Sara had not really been able to see much. The windows in the airplane were so high, and every time she got up on her knees to get her face closer to the window for a better view, her father had told her to sit back down and buckle her seat belt. She really did not have much fun that day.

But this was very different. She could see everything. She could see every street and building in her town. She could see the few tiny businesses sprawled out along Main Street...Hoyt's Grocery Store, and Pete's Drug Store and the Post Office....She could see her beautiful river winding its way through the town. And a few cars were moving about and a handful of people were walking here and there.

"Oh, Solomon," Sara said breathlessly, "this is the absolute best thing that has ever happened to me. Let's go to my school, Solomon. I'll show you where I spend my da...." Sara's voice trailed off as she sped off toward her school.

"The school looks so different from up here!" Sara was surprised at how large her school looked. The roof seemed like it went on forever. "Wow!" Sara exclaimed. "Can we go down closer, or do we have to stay way up here?"

You may go wherever you want to go, Sara.

Sara squealed, once again, and swooped down over the playground and slowly past her classroom window. "This is great! Look, Solomon! You can see my desk, and there's Mr. Jorgensen."

Sara and Solomon soared from one end of Sara's town to the other, swooping down close to the ground and then soaring back up, almost touching the clouds. "Look, Solomon, there's Jason and Billy."

"Hey, Jason, look at me, I'm flying!" Sara shouted. But Jason did not hear. "Hey, Jason!" Sara shouted again, more loudly. "Look at me! I'm flying!"

Jason cannot hear you, Sara.

"But why not? I can hear him."

It's too soon for Jason, Sara. He's not asking yet. But he will. In time.

Now Sara understood, more clearly, why Jason and Billy had not yet spotted Solomon. "They can't see you, either, can they, Solomon?"

Sara was glad that Jason and Billy could not see Solomon. *They would really get in the way, if they could,* she thought.

Sara could not ever remember having a more wonderful time. She soared high into the sky, so high that the cars on Main Street looked like little ants moving about. And then, with what felt like no effort at all, she would swoop way down, very close to the ground, squealing as she felt the amazing speed of her flight. She swooped down right over the river with her face so close to the water she could smell the sweet mossy smell, ducked right under the Main Street Bridge and then zoomed out the other side. Solomon kept perfect pace with her, as if they had practiced this flight hundreds of times.

They soared for what seemed like hours, and then, with the same powerful whoosh that sent Sara soaring upward, she was back into her body, and back on the ground.

Sara was so excited, she could barely catch her breath. This had truly been the most exceptional experience of her lifetime. "Oh, Solomon, that was wonderful!" Sara squealed. It felt to Sara as if they had been flying for hours.

"What time is it?" Sara blurted, looking at her watch, certain that she would be in big trouble for being so tardy today, but her watch showed that only a few seconds had passed.

"Solomon, you live a very strange life, you know? Nothing is quite the way it is supposed to be."

What do you mean, Sara?

"Well, like we can go flying all around town, and no time passes. Don't you find that strange? And like me being able to see you, and talk to you, but Jason and Billy cannot see you, or talk to you. Don't you find that strange?"

If their wanting were strong enough, they could, Sara, or if my wanting were strong enough, I could influence their wanting.

"What do you mean?"

It was their enthusiasm for something they had not actually seen, that brought you to my thicket. They were a very important link in the unfolding of our meeting.

"Yea, I guess." Sara was not really wanting to give her little brother the credit for this extraordinary experience. She was more comfortable in letting him keep his position as a thorn in her side. But a key to her joyful enlightenment? That was too much of a stretch, just yet.

So, Sara, tell me, what you have learned today? Solomon smiled.

"I've learned that I can fly all over town and no time will pass?" Sara stated, questioningly, wondering if that was what Solomon wanted to hear. "I've learned that Jason and Billy can't hear me or see me when I fly, because they're too young, or not ready? I've learned that it isn't cold at all up there, when you fly?"

*That is all very good, and we can talk all about that later, but, Sara, did you notice, that as long as you were talking about what you **didn't** want, that you couldn't get what you **did** want? But when you began talking about what you did want — even more importantly, when you were able to begin **feeling** what you did want — then it came, instantly?*

Sara was quiet, trying to remember back. But it was not easy to think about anything that she was thinking or feeling before she was flying. She would much rather think about the flying part.

Sara, ponder this as often as you can, and practice it as much as you can.

"You want me to practice flying? All right!"

*Not just flying, Sara. **I want you to practice thinking about what you do want, and thinking about why you***

want what you want — *until you are able to really feel it. That is the most important thing you will learn from me, Sara. Have fun with this.*

And with that, Solomon was up and away.

This is the best day of my life! Sara thought. *Today, I learned to fly!*

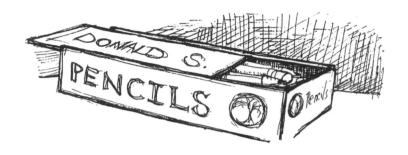

CHAPTER TEN

"Hey, baby, do you still wet the bed at night?"
Sara felt angry as she watched them mocking
Donald. Too shy to interfere, she tried to look away and not
notice what was going on.

"They think they are so smart," Sara murmured under
her breath. "They are just plain mean."

Two "too cool to be alive" boys from her classroom, who
were almost always seen together, were making fun of
Donald, a new boy, who had only been in the classroom a

couple of days. His family had just moved into town and was renting the old run-down house at the end of the street that Sara lived on. The house had been empty for months, and Sara's mother was happy to see someone finally moving in. Sara had noticed the rickety old truck being unloaded and had wondered if the little bit of broken down furniture was really all that they had.

It's hard enough to be new in town and not know any-one, but to have these verbal bullies picking on him already, well, that was just too much. Standing there in the hallway, watching Lynn and Tommy deliberately making Donald feel bad, Sara's eyes filled with tears. She re-membered the outburst of laughter in her classroom yes-terday when Donald was asked to stand to be introduced to his new classmates, and when he stood up he was clasping a bright red plastic pencil box. Sara admitted it was not the most cool thing to do. More appropriate for those of her little brother's age, but she certainly didn't believe that it deserved this kind of humiliation.

Sara realized that that had been the critical turning point for Donald. Had he been able to handle that first moment differently, perhaps standing, bravely, and grinning back, not caring what the rotten class thought about him, maybe things could have gotten off on a differ-ent foot. But that was not to be. For Donald, embarrassed, and truly frightened, slumped into his chair, biting his lip. Sara's teacher had reprimanded the class, but that really made no difference at all. The class did not seem to care what Mr. Jorgensen thought of them, but Donald surely did care what the class thought of him.

When he left the classroom, yesterday, Sara had seen him drop his bright new pencil holder into the wastebasket by the door. Once Donald was out of sight, Sara had retrieved his ill-chosen trinket and had stuffed it into her school bag.

Sara watched as Tommy and Lynn went down the hallway. She listened to hear them clumping down the stairs. She could see Donald in front of his locker, just standing there, staring into it, as if there must be something in there that would make things better, somehow, or as if he would like to crawl into the locker and avoid what is out here. Sara felt sick to her stomach. She didn't know what to do, but she wanted to do something to make Donald feel better. After looking down the hallway, to make sure the bullies were really gone, she pulled the red box from her bag and hurried toward Donald who was now fussing around with his books, in an ill at ease attempt to regain his composure.

"Hey, Donald. I saw you drop this, yesterday," Sara said, simply. "I think it's neat. I think you should keep it."

"No, I don't want it!" Donald snapped back.

Shocked, Sara stepped back and mentally tried to regain her balance.

"If you think it's so neat, you keep it!" Donald shouted at Sara.

Quickly stuffing it back into her bag, hoping no one

had seen or heard this embarrassing interchange, Sara hurried into the school yard and headed home.

"Why don't I stay out of things?" Sara scolded herself. "Why don't I learn?"

CHAPTER ELEVEN

"Solomon, why are people so mean?" Sara pleaded.

Are all people mean, Sara? I hadn't noticed.

"Well, not all of them, but lots of them are, and I don't understand why. When I'm mean, I feel awful."

When are you mean, Sara?

"Mostly when someone is mean first. I think I sort of just get mean to pay them back."

Does that help?

"Yes." Sara offered defensively.

How so, Sara? Does paying them back make you feel better? Does it turn things around, or take any meanness back?

"Well, no, I guess not."

In fact, Sara, what I have seen is that it just adds more meanness to the world. It's a bit like joining their chain-of-pain. They are hurting, and then you are hurting, and then you help someone to hurt, and on and on it goes.

"But Solomon, who started this awful chain-of-pain?"

It doesn't really matter where it started, Sara. But it IS important what you do with it if it comes to you. What is this all about, Sara? What has caused you to join this chain-of-pain?

Sara, feeling rather sick to her stomach, told Solomon about the new boy, Donald, and of his first day in class. She told Solomon about the bullies who seemed to find never-ending things to tease Donald about. She told Solomon about this alarming incident that had just taken place in the hallway. And as she re-lived these incidents, as she was describing them to Solomon, she felt her painful anger growing again, and a tear pushed out of her eye and rolled down her cheek. She angrily wiped it away with the back of her sleeve, truly irritated that instead of her usual happy chatter with Solomon, she was now sniffling and blubbering. This was not the way it was supposed to be with Solomon.

Solomon was quiet for a long while as scattered, disconnected thoughts shot about Sara's mind. Sara could feel Solomon watching her with his big loving eyes, but she did not feel self-conscious. It almost felt as if Solomon was drawing something out of her.

*Well, it's clear what I **don't** want,* Sara thought. *I don't want to feel like this. Especially when I'm talking with Solomon.*

*That's very good, Sara. You have just, consciously, taken the first step in ending the chain-of-pain. You have consciously recognized what you **do not** want.*

"And that's good?" Sara questioned. "It doesn't feel so good."

That's only because you have only taken the first step, Sara. There are three more.

"What is the next step, Solomon?"

Well, Sara, it isn't hard to figure out what you don't want. Do you agree with that?

"Yes, I guess I do. I mean, I think I usually know that."

*How do you know that you are thinking about what you **don't** want?*

"I can just sorta tell."

*You can tell by the way you feel, Sara. When you are thinking about, or speaking about, something that you **do not** want — you always feel negative emotion. You feel anger, or disappointment, or embarrassment, or guilt, or fear. You always feel bad when you are thinking about something you **do not** want.*

Sara thought back over the last few days, during which she had experienced more negative emotion than usual. "You are right, Solomon," Sara announced, "I have been feeling more of that, this last week, watching those boys being mean to Donald. I've been so happy since meeting you, Solomon, and then so mad about them teasing Donald. I can see how the way I feel has to do with what I am thinking about."

*Good, Sara. Now, let's talk about step two. Whenever you know what you **don't** want, isn't it rather easy to figure out what you **do** want?*

"Well....." Sara trailed off, wanting to understand, but still unsure.

When you are sick, what is it that you then want?

"I want to feel better," Sara replied easily.

When you don't have enough money to buy something that you want, then what do you want?

"I want more money," Sara replied.

*You see, Sara, that is step two of breaking the chain-of-pain. Step one is recognizing what you **don't** want. Step two is then deciding what you **do** want.*

"Well, that's easy enough." Sara was beginning to feel better.

Step three is the most important step, Sara, and it is the step that most people miss altogether. Step three is this: Once you have identified what it is that you do want, you must make that feel real. You must talk about why you want it, describe what it would be like to have it, explain it, pretend it, or remember another time like it — but keep thinking about it until you find that feeling place. Continue to talk to yourself about what it is that you do want until you feel good.

As Sara listened to Solomon actually encouraging her to spend time, on purpose, imagining things in her own mind, she could hardly believe her ears. She had gotten into serious trouble for that very thing on more than one occasion. It seemed that what Solomon was telling her was exactly opposite of what her teachers in school were telling her. But she had come to trust Solomon. And she was certainly willing to try something different. Their way, obviously, was not working.

"Why is step three the most important step, Solomon?"

Because, until you change the way you feel, you haven't really changed anything. You are still part of the chain-of-pain. But when you change the way you feel, you are part of a different chain. You have joined Solomon's chain, so to speak.

"What do you call your chain, Solomon?"

Well, I don't really call it anything. It is more about feeling it. But you might call it the Chain-of-Joy, or the Chain-of-Well-being. The Chain-of-Feeling-Good. It is the natural chain, Sara. It is truly who we all are.

"Well, if it's natural, if it's who we all are, why aren't more of us feeling good more of the time?"

People truly want to feel good, and most people want, very much, to be good. And that is a big part of the problem.

"What do you mean? How can wanting to be good, be a problem?"

Well, Sara, people want to be good, and so they look around them, at the way others are living, in order to decide what is good. They look at the conditions that surround them, and they see things that they believe are good and they see things that they believe are bad.

"And that is bad? I don't see what is bad about that, Solomon."

What I have noticed, Sara, is that as they are looking at conditions, good ones and bad ones, most people are not aware of how they are feeling. And that is what goes wrong for most of them. Rather than being aware of how what they are looking at is affecting them, in their quest for goodness, they keep searching out badness and trying to push that away. The trouble with that, Sara, is that the whole time they are trying to push away what they think is bad — they have joined the chain-of-pain. People are much more interested in looking at and analyzing and comparing conditions than they are aware of how they are feeling. And often the condition drags them right off into the chain-of-pain.

Sara, think back over the past few days, and try to remember some of the strong feelings that you had. What was happening as you were feeling bad this week, Sara?

"I felt awful when Tommy and Lynn were teasing Donald. I felt awful when the kids laughed at Donald in class, and I felt the very worst of all when Donald yelled at me. All I was trying to do was help him, Solomon."

Good, Sara. Let's talk about this. During those times that you were feeling so bad, what were you doing?

"I don't know, Solomon. I wasn't really doing anything. I was mostly just watching, I guess."

That is exactly right, Sara. You were observing conditions — but the conditions that you were choosing to observe were the kind that make you join the chain-of-pain.

"But Solomon," Sara argued. "How can you not see something that is wrong and not feel bad when you see it?"

That's a very good question, Sara, and I promise you that in time I will answer it fully for you. I know it is not easy to understand this all at once. And the reason that it is difficult to understand, at first, is because you have been trained to observe conditions, but you have not been trained to pay attention to how you feel when you are observing — and so, the conditions seem to control your lives. If you are observing something good, you have a good feeling response, and if you are observing something bad, you have a bad feeling response. When the conditions seem to control your lives, that is frustrating for most of you, and that is what causes so many people to continue to join the chain-of-pain.

"Then, how can I stay out of the chain-of-pain, so that I can help someone else out, if they get in?"

Well, Sara, there are lots of ways to do that. But my favorite — the one that works the very fastest of all — is this: Think thoughts of appreciation.

"Appreciation?"

Yes, Sara, focus on something, or someone, and try to find thoughts that make you feel the very best. Appreciate them just as much as you can. That is the very best way to join the Chain-of-Joy.

Remember, Step One is?

"Knowing what I *don't* want," Sara answered proudly. She had that one down pat.

And Step Two is?

"Knowing what I *do* want."

That's very good, Sara. And Step Three is?

"Oh, Solomon, I forget," Sara whined, disappointed at herself for forgetting so soon.

Step three is finding the feeling place of what you do want. *Talking about what you do want until you feel like you are already there.*

"Solomon, you never told me what Step Four is," Sara remembered, excitedly.

Ah, Step Four is the best part, Sara. That is when you get what you want. **Step Four is the physical manifestation of your desire.**

Have fun with this, Sara. Don't try too hard to remember all of this. **Just practice appreciation. That's the key.** *You'd better run along now, Sara. We can talk more about this tomorrow.*

Appreciation, Sara pondered. *I will try to think of things to appreciate.* Her little brother, Jason, was the first image that came to her mind. *Boy, this is going to be hard,* Sara thought, as she began walking from Solomon's thicket.

Start with something easier! Solomon called as he lifted from his post.

"Yea, right," Sara laughed. *I love you, Solomon,* Sara thought.

I love you too, Sara. Sara heard Solomon's voice, clearly, even though he had flown far from her view.

CHAPTER TWELVE

Something easy, Sara thought, *I want to appreciate something easy.*

From a distance, Sara could see her next door neighbor's dog frolicking in the snow. He was leaping and running, then rolling on his back, obviously happy to be alive.

Brownie, you are such a happy dog! I do appreciate you, Sara thought, still over 200 yards away. At that moment, Brownie began running toward Sara as if she were his master and had called his name. Wagging his tail, he ran two full circles around Sara, and then, with his paws on her shoulders, this large, mangy, long-haired dog pushed Sara into a sitting position into the pile of snow that was left by the snow plow earlier that week — and he licked her face with his warm wet tongue. Sara was laughing so hard she could barely get up. "Oh, you love me, too, do you, Brownie?"

Sara lay in her bed that night, thinking about everything that had happened that week. *I feel like I've been on a roller coaster. I've felt the best I have ever felt and the worst I have ever felt, all in one short week. I love my talks with Solomon, and, oh, how I loved learning to fly, but I got so mad this week, too. This is all very strange.*

Think thoughts of appreciation. Sara could have sworn she heard Solomon's voice in her bedroom.

"No, that cannot be," Sara decided. "I'm just remembering what Solomon said." And with that, Sara rolled over onto her side, to ponder. *I appreciate this nice warm bed, that's for sure,* Sara thought, as she tugged the blankets up over her shoulders. *And my pillow. My soft, snuggly pillow. I do appreciate this,* Sara thought, wrapping her arms around it and burying her face in it. *I appreciate my mother and my father. And Jas...... And Jason, too.*

I don't know, Sara thought. *I don't think I'm finding that feeling place. Maybe I'm just too tired. I'll work on this tomorrow.* And with that last conscious thought, Sara was sound asleep.

"I'm flying again! I'm flying again!" Sara shouted, as she soared high above her house. *Flying isn't exactly the best word for this,* she thought. *More like floating. I can go any-where I want to go!*

With no effort at all, but just by identifying where she wanted to be, Sara moved easily across the sky, pausing now and then to examine something she had not noticed before, sometimes swooping very close to the ground, and then lifting back up again. Up! Up! Up! She discovered that if she wanted to go down, all she had to do was stretch one toe toward the ground and down she would go. When she was ready to go back up again, she just looked upward, and up she would go.

I want to fly forever and ever! Sara decided.

Let's see, Sara puzzled, *where should I go now?* Sara moved along, way up over her little town, seeing lights blinking off, here and there, as family after family, house after house, settled in for the night. It was beginning to snow, very lightly, and Sara thrilled at how warm and secure she felt, floating about in the middle of the night in her bare feet and flannel nightgown. *It's not cold at all,* Sara noticed.

Nearly every house was dark, now, and only the town's sparsely placed street lights were glowing, but on the far side of town, Sara could see one house still lighted. And so, she decided to go there to see who was still up. *Probably somebody who doesn't have to get up early in the morning,* Sara thought, getting closer, and stretching her left toe down-ward, causing a perfect and rapid descent.

She dropped down to a small kitchen window, glad that the curtains were open so she could peek inside. And there, sitting at the kitchen table, with papers spread all over the

place, was Mr. Jorgensen, Sara's teacher. Mr. Jorgensen was methodically picking up one paper, reading it, then another, then another....Sara was transfixed as she watched him. He seemed to be so serious about whatever he was doing.

Sara began to feel a little bit guilty, spying on her teacher like this. *But at least this is the kitchen window,* Sara noted, *not the bathroom, or bedroom, or something private like that.*

Now Mr. Jorgensen was smiling, seeming to really enjoy whatever he was reading. Now he was writing something on it. And then, suddenly, Sara realized what Mr. Jorgensen was doing. He was reading the papers Sara's class had turned in at the end of the day. He was reading every single one of them.

Sara had often found something scrawled on the top or the back of the papers he had returned to her, and she had never much appreciated it. *You just can't please him,* Sara had thought, many times, as she read his scribbled notes on her papers.

But watching this man, reading, then writing, reading and then writing, while most everyone else in town was now fast asleep, left Sara feeling very strange. She felt almost dizzy as her old negative perspective of Mr. Jorgensen and her very new perspective of Mr. Jorgensen had a sort of collision inside her head. "Wow!" Sara said, as she looked upward, causing her little body to zoom up high above her teacher's house.

A warm gust of wind seemed to come from inside Sara, wrapping all around her body and giving her goose bumps on her skin. Her eyes filled with tears and her heart leaped a happy beat and she soared, ever so high, into the sky and looked down upon her beautiful, sleeping, or almost sleeping, town.

I feel appreciation for you, Mr. Jorgensen, Sara thought as she made one last swoop over his house and headed home. And as Sara looked back at Mr. Jorgensen's kitchen window, she felt sure that she saw him standing there, looking out.

CHAPTER THIRTEEN

"Hi, Mr. Matson," Sara heard her own voice ring out as she crossed the Main Street Bridge on her way to school.

Mr. Matson looked up from under the hood of the car he was working on. He had seen Sara on her way to school hundreds of mornings throughout the years that he had operated the town's one and only gas station on the corner of Main Street and Center Street, but she had never called out to him that way before. He really didn't know quite how to respond, and so, he waved a sort of half wave, in his surprise. In fact, most people who knew Sara, were beginning to notice startling differences in her usually introverted behavior. Instead of looking down, watching her feet and deep in her own thoughts, Sara was strangely interested in her mountain town, unusually observant and amazingly interactive.

"So many things to appreciate!" Sara was acknowledging, quietly, under her breath. *The snow plow has already cleared most of the streets. That's really a nice thing,* Sara thought. *I do appreciate that.*

She saw a utility truck in front of Bergman's Store with its extension ladder extended all the way out. One man was at the very top of the ladder, working at the top of a power pole, while another man watched intently from down below. Sara wondered what they were doing, and decided they were probably repairing one of the power lines that had become too heavy with the heavy icicles that were clinging to it. *That's really nice,* Sara thought. *It is so nice that these men are able to keep our electricity working. I do appreciate that.*

A school bus, filled with children, rounded the corner as Sara walked into the school yard. Sara couldn't see any of their faces because the windows were all fogged up, but she was very familiar with the routine: The bus driver, who had been gathering his unwilling cargo from all over the county since before dawn, was now releasing about half of them at Sara's school. He would unload the other half at Sara's old school down on Main Street. *That is a nice thing that the bus driver does,* Sara thought. *I really do appreciate that.*

Sara took off her heavy coat as she walked inside the school building, noticing how comfortably warm it felt inside. *I do appreciate this building, and the furnace that keeps it warm, and the janitor who tends the furnace.* She remembered watching him shoveling chunks of coal into the bin that would feed the fire for a few more hours, and she had seen him removing the big red clinkers from the furnace. *I appreciate this janitor who does his job to keep us warm.*

Sara was feeling wonderful. *I'm really catching on to this appreciation stuff,* she thought. *I wonder why I haven't figured this out sooner. This is great!*

"Hey, Baby Face!" Sara heard a contrived whiny voice taunting someone. The words felt so awful, Sara winced as she heard them. It was shocking to come from a place of feeling soooo wonderful to this sickening realization that someone was picking on someone.

Oh, no, Sara thought, *not Donald again.* But, sure enough, the same two bullies were at it again. They had Donald cornered in the hallway. His body was pressed up against his locker, and Sara could see Lynn and Tommy's grinning faces only inches from his.

Suddenly, Sara was not shy at all. "Why don't you goons find someone your own size to pick on?" Well, that was not exactly what Sara meant to say, since Donald was actually quite a bit taller than either of them, but the confidence that they seemed to gather from always running in packs, left Donald, or whoever they were picking on at the moment, at a seeming disadvantage.

"Oh, Donald's got a girl friend, Donald's got a girl friend," the boys chanted in unison. Sara's face flushed red with embarrassment and then redder with anger.

The boys laughed and moved on down the hallway, leaving Sara standing there, flushed and feeling very hot and uncomfortable.

"I don't need you to stick up for me!" Donald shouted, again blasting anger at Sara, to conceal his tears of embarrassment.

Good grief, Sara thought. *I'm doing it again. I just don't learn.*

Well, Donald, Sara thought, *I appreciate you, too. You have, once again, helped me to realize that I am an idiot. An idiot who does not learn.*

CHAPTER FOURTEEN

"Hi, Solomon," Sara offered flatly, hanging her book bag over the post next to Solomon's post.

Good day, Sara. It is a beautiful day. Do you agree?

"Yes, I guess it is." Sara replied, blankly, not really noticing, or even caring, that the sun was shining brightly again. Sara loosened her neck scarf and tugged it from around her neck, stuffing it into her pocket.

Solomon waited, quietly, for Sara to gather her thoughts and begin her usual barrage of questions, but Sara was unusually sullen today.

"Solomon," Sara began. "I don't get it."

What is it that you do not understand, Sara?

"I don't understand what good it does anybody for me to go around appreciating things. I mean, I really don't see what good it is doing."

What do you mean, Sara?

"Well, I mean, I was getting pretty good at it. I've been practicing it all week. At first it was pretty hard, but then it got easier. And today, I was appreciating just about everything, until I got to school and heard Lynn and Tommy picking on poor Donald, again."

Then what happened?

"Then I got mad. I got so mad I yelled at them. I just wanted them to leave Donald alone, so that he can be happy. But I did it again, Solomon. I joined their chain-of-pain. I haven't learned anything. I just hate those boys, Solomon. I think they are awful."

Why do you hate them?

"Because they ruined my perfect day. All of this day I was going to appreciate things. When I woke up this morning, I appreciated my bed, and then my breakfast, and my mother and father, and even Jason. And all the way to school I found so many things to appreciate, and then they ruined it, Solomon. They made me feel awful again. Like before. Just like before I learned how to appreciate."

It's no wonder you are mad at them, Sara, for you are in a terrible trap. In fact, that is just about the worst trap in the world.

Sara didn't much like the sound of that. She had seen enough of Jason and Billy's home-made traps, and had freed many little mice and squirrels and birds that they had gleefully captured. The idea of someone putting her in a trap made Sara feel awful. "What do you mean, Solomon? What trap?"

Well, Sara, when your happiness depends on what somebody else does or does not do, you are trapped, because you cannot control what they think or what they do. But, Sara, you will discover true liberation — a freedom beyond your wildest dreams — when you discover that your joy does not depend on anyone else. Your joy only depends on what YOU choose to give your attention to.

Sara listened, quietly, with tears running down her pink cheeks.

You feel trapped, right now, because you don't see how you could respond differently to what you saw happen. As you witness something that makes you feel uncomfortable — you are responding to those conditions. And you think that the only way you can feel better is if the conditions are better. And since you cannot control the conditions, you feel trapped.

Sara wiped her face with her sleeve. She felt very uncomfortable. Solomon was right. She did feel trapped. And she wanted to be free of the trap.

Sara, just keep working on appreciating — and you'll begin to feel better. We'll sort this out a little bit at a time. You'll see. This will not be difficult for you to understand. Keep having fun. We'll talk more, tomorrow. Sleep well.

CHAPTER FIFTEEN

Solomon was right. Things did seem to just get better and better. In fact, the next few weeks were the best Sara could ever remember. Everything seemed to be going so well. The school days seemed to be getting shorter and shorter, and, to Sara's surprise, she was actually beginning to like school. But Solomon continued to be the very best part of Sara's day.

"Solomon," Sara said, "I'm so glad that I found you here in this thicket. You are my best friend."

I'm glad, too, Sara. We are birds of a feather, you know?

"Well, you are half right, anyway," Sara laughed, looking at Solomon's beautiful coat of feathers and feeling that warm wind of appreciation flowing through her. She had heard her mother say, "Birds of a feather flock together," but she had never thought much about what it meant, and she certainly never expected that she would ever find herself flocking with birds.

"What does that mean, anyway, Solomon?"

People use that expression to point out their awareness that things that are like one another come together. That which is like unto itself is drawn.

"You mean, like robins stay together, and crows stay together, and squirrels stay together?"

Well, yes, like that. But really, all things that are alike do that, Sara. But the likeness is not always what you think it is. It's not usually something obvious that you can see.

"I don't understand, Solomon. If you can't see it, how do you know that they are alike or different?"

You can feel it, Sara. But it takes practice, and before you can practice, you have to know what you are looking for, and, since most people don't understand the basic rules, they don't know what to look for.

"Rules, like in rules of a game, Solomon?"

Yes, sort of like that. Actually, a better name would be 'Law of Attraction.' **Law of Attraction says, 'That which is like unto itself is drawn.'**

"Oh, I see," Sara brightened. "Like birds of a feather flock together."

That's it, Sara. And everyone and everything in the entire Universe is affected by this Law.

"I still don't really understand this, Solomon. Tell me more, please."

Tomorrow, as you are moving through your day, watch for the evidence of this Law. Keep your eyes and ears open, and, most importantly, pay attention to the way that you feel as you observe things and people and animals and situations around you. Have fun with this, Sara. We'll talk more about it, tomorrow.

Hmmm, Birds of a feather, flock together, Sara pondered. And as those words rolled across her mind, a large flock of geese flushed up from the pasture and flapped above Sara's head. Sara had always loved watching these winter geese, and she was always amazed at the patterns they made as they flew across the sky. Sara laughed at the seeming coincidence of talking about flocking birds and then immediately finding the sky filled with them. *Hmmm, Law of Attraction!*

CHAPTER SIXTEEN

Mr. Pack's shiny old Buick slowed down as it passed Sara. Sara waved at Mr. and Mrs. Pack, and they smiled and waved back.

Sara remembered her father's comments about their elderly neighbors. "Those old geezers are just alike."

"They even seem to look alike," her mother had added.

Hmmm, Sara pondered, *they are awfully much alike.* Sara thought back over the time she had known these neighbors. "They are both as neat as a button," her mother had noticed right from the beginning. Mr. Pack's car was always the

shiniest in town. "He must wash it every day," Sara's father
had groaned, not appreciating the contrast that Mr. Pack's,
always clean, car struck with his own, usually dirty, one.
Mr. Pack's summer lawn and gardens were always trimmed
and planted to perfection, and Mrs. Pack was every bit as
tidy as her husband. Sara did not have much opportunity
to be inside their house, but on the rare occasion that she
had run an errand for her mother, that had taken her inside,
Sara was always impressed with the house, always tidy and
clean, never even one thing out of place. *Ah, Law of
Attraction,* Sara concluded.

Sara's brother, Jason, and his rambunctious friend, Billy,
sped by Sara on their bicycles, each coming as close to Sara
as possible without actually bumping her. "Hey, Sara, better watch where you're going," Jason chided. Sara could
hear them laughing as they raced down the road.

Brats! Sara thought, as she reclaimed her place back on
the roadway, irritated that she had scrambled so to get out
of their way. "They were made for each other," Sara grumbled. "They take such delight in making trouble." Sara
stopped dead in her tracks. "Birds of a feather," Sara
brightened. "They are birds of a feather! This is Law of
Attraction!"

And everyone and everything in the Universe is affected by it!
Sara remembered Solomon's words.

The next day, Sara spent as much time as possible looking for evidence of Law of Attraction.

It's everywhere! Sara concluded, as she observed adults
and children and teenagers moving about her town.

Sara stopped at Hoyt's Store, a sort of general store right in the middle of town and only slightly out of Sara's way to school. She bought a new eraser to replace the one some- one had borrowed yesterday and had not returned, and a candy bar to eat after lunch.

Sara had always liked coming into this store. It always felt good. The store was owned by three cheerful men who were always ready and willing to play with whoever walked into the store. It was always a very busy place, since it was the only grocery store in town, but even when the lines were long, these three men managed to joke and kid with anyone who was willing to play along.

"How's it going, Kiddo?" the taller of the three quipped at Sara.

His enthusiasm startled Sara a bit. They had never played much with Sara, which had always suited Sara just fine, but today, they clearly intended to make Sara part of their fun.

"It's going fine." Sara replied boldly.

"Well, that's what I like to hear! Which are you going to eat first, the candy bar or the eraser?"

"I thought I'd eat the candy bar first. I'll save the eraser for dessert!" Sara grinned back at him.

Mr. Hoyt laughed hard. Sara had truly taken him off guard with her quick humor. Sara's clever reply had surprised Sara, too.

"Well, you have a good day, Sweetheart! Keep having fun!"

Sara felt wonderful as she walked back out onto Main Street. *Birds of a feather,* Sara pondered. *Law of Attraction. It's everywhere!*

What a beautiful day! Sara appreciated, leaning back, looking upward at the bright blue sky, on this exceptionally warm winter day. The usually frozen streets and sidewalks were shining wet, and little streams of water were trickling across Sara's path, forming little puddles here and there.

"Varoooooom," Jason and Billy yelled in unison as they whizzed past Sara, riding their bicycles as fast and as close to her as they could without bumping into her. Dirty water splashed up Sara's legs.

"Monsters!" Sara yelled, dripping with muddy water and seething with anger. *This just doesn't make sense. I've got to ask Solomon about this.*

Her wet clothes dried and most of the muddy marks were brushed away, but by the end of the day Sara was still confused and angry. She was mad at Jason, but then there was nothing new in that. Sara felt angry at Solomon, too, and at Law of Attraction and Birds of a Feather and at mean people. In fact, Sara was pretty much mad at everybody.

As always, Solomon was perched on his post, waiting patiently for Sara's visit.

You seem unusually excited today, Sara. What is it you are wanting to talk about?

"Solomon!" Sara blurted, "Something is wrong with this Law of Attraction thing!"

Sara waited, expecting Solomon to correct her.

Go on, Sara.

"Well, you said that the Law of Attraction says that that which is like unto itself is drawn? And Jason and Billy are really rotten, Solomon. They spend all day, mostly, looking for ways to make other people feel bad." Sara paused a bit, still expecting Solomon to interrupt.

Go on.

"Well, Solomon, I'm not rotten. I mean, I don't splash mud on people or bump them with my bicycle. I don't trap or kill little animals or let the air out of people's tires, so how come Jason and Billy keep flocking with me? We aren't birds of a feather, Solomon. We are different!"

Do you think that Jason and Billy are truly rotten, Sara?

"Yes, Solomon, I do!"

They are rascals, I'll agree with you there, Solomon smiled, *but they are pretty much like everyone and everything in the universe. They have that which is wanted, and lack of it, all mixed in together. Have you ever noticed your brother doing something nice?*

"Well, yes, I guess. But hardly ever." Sara stammered. "I'd have to think about that. But, Solomon, I still don't get it. How come they keep bothering me? I don't bother them!"

Well, Sara, this is the way that it works. In every moment, you have the option of looking at something that you want, or at the lack of it. When you are looking at something you want — just by observing it, you begin to vibrate as it is. You become the same as it is, Sara, do you understand?

"You mean that just by watching someone who is rotten, I am rotten too?"

Well, not exactly, but you are beginning to understand. Imagine a light board, about the size of your bed.

"A light board?"

*Yes, Sara. A board with thousands of little lights, like little Christmas tree lights, protruding up from the board. A sea of lights. Thousands of them, and you are one of these lights. When you give your attention to something, just by giving it your attention, your light on the board lights up, and, in that moment, every other light on the board — **that is in vibrational harmony with your light** — lights up, too. And those lighted lights represent your world. Those are the people and experiences that you now have vibrational access to.*

Think about it, Sara. Of all the people you know, who does your brother, Jason, tease and harass the most?

Sara answered instantly. "Me, Solomon. He is always bothering me!"

And of all the people you know, who do you think is most bothered by Jason's teasing? Who do you think lights their light board in vibrational harmony with these rascals, Sara?

Sara laughed, now beginning to understand. "It's me, Solomon. I am most bothered. I keep lighting my light board by watching Jason and getting mad at him."

So, you see, Sara, as you see something you do not like, and you notice it and push against it and think about it — you light your light board, and then you get more of that. Often, you are vibrating there even when Jason is nowhere around. You are just remembering the last thing that happened when he <u>was</u> around. The nice thing about all of this, Sara, is this: You can always tell, by the way you are feeling, what you are achieving vibrational harmony with.

"What do you mean?"

*Whenever you are happy, whenever you are feeling appreciation, whenever you are noticing the positive aspects of someone or something, you are vibrating in harmony with what you **do** want. But whenever you feel angry or fearful, whenever you feel guilty or disappointed, you are — in that very moment — achieving harmony with what you **do not** want.*

"Every single time, Solomon?"

*Yes. Every time. You can always trust the way you feel. It is your Guidance System. Ponder this, Sara. In the next few days, as you are observing those around you, pay particular attention to the way you are feeling. Show yourself, Sara, what **you** are achieving vibrational harmony with.*

"Okay, Solomon. I'll try. But this is pretty tricky, you know. This may take a lot of practice."

Agreed. It's nice that there are so many others around you to give you an opportunity to practice. Have fun with this.

And with that, Solomon was up and away.

Easy for you to say, Solomon, Sara thought. *You get to choose who you spend time with. You are not stuck in school with Lynn and Tommy. You don't have to live with Jason.*

Then, as clearly as if Solomon were sitting right there speaking directly into Sara's ears, she heard: *When your happiness depends on what somebody else does or does not do, you are trapped, because you cannot control what they think or what they do. You will discover a true liberation, a freedom beyond your wildest dreams, when you discover that your joy does not depend on anyone else.* **Your joy only depends on what <u>you</u> choose to give your attention to.**

CHAPTER SEVENTEEN

What a day this has been, Sara pondered, as she walked towards Solomon's thicket.

"I hate school!" Sara blurted right out loud, as she slipped back into the feeling of anger that had begun the very moment she had walked onto the school grounds. She walked along, looking mostly down at her feet, recalling the details of this wretched day.

She had arrived at the front gate at the same moment that the school bus arrived, and when the bus driver opened the doors, a herd of rowdy boys had almost mowed Sara down, bumping her from every direction, causing her to drop her books, spilling the contents of her bag. And worst of all, her theme paper for Mr. Jorgensen had been literally trampled. Sara gathered the crumpled, muddied papers into a pile and stuffed them into her bag. "That's what I get for caring what the stupid paper looks like," Sara had grumbled, regretting, now, having taken the time to re-write it a second time before folding it carefully and putting it into her book bag.

Still trying to get things back together as she walked through the big front doors, Sara was not moving fast enough for Miss Webster. "Move along, Sara, I haven't got all day!" the slender, and mostly hated, third grade teacher had snapped at Sara.

"Excuse me for being alive!" Sara had muttered under her breath. "Good grief!"

Sara must have looked at her watch 100 times this day, counting the minutes to some freedom from this rampage of meanness.

And then, at last, the final bell, and Sara was free.

"I hate school. I really hate school. How can something that feels so terrible be of any value to anyone?"

Out of habit, Sara made her way to Solomon's thicket, and as she made the last turn onto Thacker's Trail, Sara thought, *This is the very worst mood I've been in, ever. Especially since meeting Solomon.*

"Solomon," Sara complained, "I hate school. I think it is a waste of time."

Solomon was very quiet.

"It's like a cage that you can't get out of, and the people in the cage are mean and looking for ways to hurt you, all day long."

Still, no comment from Solomon.

"It's bad enough when the kids are mean to each other, but the teachers are mean, too, Solomon. I don't think they like being there, either."

Solomon just sat there, staring. Only the occasional blinking of his big yellow eyes let Sara know that he was not sound asleep.

A tear slipped down Sara's cheek as her frustration welled up within her. "Solomon, I just want to be happy. And I don't think I will ever be happy at school."

Well then, Sara, I think you'd better get out of town, too.

Sara looked up, startled at Solomon's sudden comment. "What did you say, Solomon? Get out of town, too?"

Yes, Sara, if you are leaving your school because there are some negative things there, then I think you should get out of town, too, and out of this state and out of this country and off the face of this earth, even out of this universe. And now, Sara, I don't know where to send you.

Sara was confused. This did not seem like the solution-seeking Solomon she had come to know and love.

"Solomon, what are you saying?"

Well, Sara, I have discovered that in every single particle of the universe there is that which is wanted and lack of it. In every person, in every situation, in every place, in every moment — those choices are always there. Ever present. So you see, Sara, if you are

leaving one place, or circumstance, because there is negative in it,
the next place you go will be pretty much the same.

"You're not making me feel better, Solomon. It feels
hopeless."

*Sara, your work is not to look for the perfect place where only the things you want exist. Your work is to look for the things you want in **every** place.*

"But why? What good does that do?"

*Well, for one thing, you would feel better, and, for another thing, **as you begin to notice more things that you want to see, more of those things begin to become part of your experience.** It gets easier and easier, Sara.*

"But, Solomon, aren't some places a lot worse than others? I mean school is just the worst place in the world to be."

Well, Sara, it is easier to find positive things in some places than others, but that can become a pretty big trap.

"What do you mean?"

When you see something you do not like and you decide to go somewhere else to get away from it — you usually take it with you.

"But, Solomon, I wouldn't take those mean teachers or rotten kids with me."

Well, maybe not those very same ones, Sara, but you would meet others, very much like them, everywhere you would go. Sara, remember "Birds of a Feather." Remember the "Light Board." When you see things you don't like and you think about them and talk about them, you become like them, and then everywhere you go, they are there, too.

"Solomon, I keep forgetting all of this."

Well, Sara, it's natural to forget this, because you are like most people who have learned to respond to conditions. If good condi-

tions are around you, you respond by feeling good, but if there are bad conditions around you, you respond by feeling bad.

Most people think that they must first find perfect conditions, and once they find those perfect conditions, then they can respond by being happy. But that is very frustrating to people, because they discover, very soon, that they cannot control the conditions.

What you are learning, Sara, is that you are not here to find perfect conditions. You are here to choose things to appreciate — which causes you to vibrate like the perfect conditions — so that you can then attract perfect conditions.

"I guess," Sara sighed. This all seemed too big to understand.

Sara, it really isn't as complicated as it seems. In fact, people make it much more complicated as they try to make sense of all of the conditions that surround them. It can get very confusing if you are trying to figure out how every condition is created, or which conditions are right and which ones are wrong. You can drive yourself crazy trying to sort all of that out. But if you will just pay attention to whether your valve is open or closed, then your life will be much simpler and much happier.

"My valve? What do you mean?"

Sara, in every moment, a stream of pure positive energy is flowing to you. You might say it is a bit like the water pressure in your house. That water pressure is always there, right up against your valve. And when you want water in your house, you open the valve and let the water flow in. But when the valve is closed shut, the water does not flow in. It is your work to keep this valve to Well-being open. It's always there for you, but you must let it in.

"But, Solomon," Sara protested. "What good does it do for me to keep my valve open in a school where everyone else is angry and mean?"

First of all, when your valve is open, you won't notice so much of the meanness, and some of it will change right before your eyes. There are many people who are sort of teetering on the edge of an open or closed valve, and when they come into contact with you, and your valve is wide open, they eas-*ily join you in a smile, or a nice interchange. Also, you must remember that an open valve is not only affecting what is happening right now. It is affecting tomorrow and the next day. So, the more todays that you are feeling good, the more conditions of tomorrow and the next day will be pleasing to you. Practice this, Sara.*

Make a decision that no condition, no matter how bad it may seem to you in the moment, is worth your closing your valve. Decide that keeping your valve open is the most important thing.

Here are some words to remember, Sara, and to say, as often as you can: "I am going to keep my valve open, anyway."

"Well, all right, Solomon," Sara replied, meekly, feeling tentative about the whole thing, but remembering how much better things, on the whole, had been going since she had tried some of the other techniques Solomon had offered.

"I'll practice this. I hope it works," Sara called back over her shoulder as she left Solomon's thicket. *It really would be nice to be able to feel good no matter what. That really is what I want.*

CHAPTER EIGHTEEN

Sara's mother's car was in the driveway. *That's strange,* Sara thought. *She's not supposed to be home this early.*

"Hi, I'm home," Sara called out, as she opened the front door, surprising herself with such an unusual announcement of her arrival. But no answer came back. Sara put her books down on the dining room table and called again, walking through the kitchen into the hallway leading to the bedrooms, "Anybody home?"

"I'm in here, Honey," Sara heard her mother's quiet voice. The drapes in her mother's bedroom were closed, and Sara's mother was lying on her bed with a pink rolled towel across her eyes and forehead.

"What's wrong, Mom?" Sara asked.

"Oh, I just have a headache, Honey. It's been hurting all day, and finally I decided I couldn't stay at work another minute, so I came home."

"Is it better now?"

"It feels better to have my eyes closed. I'll just lie here for a little while. I'll be out later. Close the door for me, and when your brother comes home, tell him I'll be out later. Maybe if I can sleep for a little while, I'll feel better."

Sara tiptoed out of the room and gently closed the door. She stood in the dark hallway, for a bit, trying to decide what to do next. She knew what chores should be tended to, she had done those same chores every day for as long as she could remember, but everything felt different, somehow.

Sara could not remember the last time her mother had stayed home from work, sick, and there was something very unsettling about all of this. Sara had a knot in her stomach and she felt disoriented. She had not realized how her mother's usual stability and good humor had such a stabilizing influence on her own day.

"I don't like this," Sara said aloud. "I hope Mom feels better, fast."

Sara. Sara heard Solomon's voice. *Does your happiness depend on the conditions around you? This might be a good opportunity to practice.*

"Okay, Solomon. But how do I practice? What am I supposed to do?"

Just open your valve, Sara. When you feel bad, your valve is closed. So try to think thoughts that feel better until you feel your valve open up again.

Sara went out into the kitchen, but her thoughts were still mostly about her mother lying in her bed in the next room. Her mother's purse was on the kitchen table, and Sara could not stop thinking about her mother.

Make a decision to do something, Sara. Think about your chores, and decide to do them in record time, tonight. Think about doing something extra, something beyond your normal chores.

And with that idea, Sara was inspired to instant action. She moved quickly and certainly, picking up things from around the house that had been misplaced, slowly, over many hours last evening before bed time, by various members of the family. She gathered and stacked the newspapers that seemed to cover most of the living room floor, and then dusted the table tops in the living room. She cleaned the sink and the bathtub in the family's only bathroom. She emptied the garbage cans from the kitchen and the bathroom. She tidied the papers strewn across her father's great big oak desk which was awkwardly crammed in the corner of the living room, being careful not to move anything too far from where her father had placed it. She was never certain if there was order to his disorder, but she didn't want to cause any problems. Her father actually spent very little time at that desk, and Sara often wondered why such a big piece of the living room had to be devoted to it. But it seemed to give her father a place to think, and, more importantly, a place to stash things he didn't want to think about right now.

She was moving quickly, with strong decided purpose, and it was not until she made the decision not to use the vacuum cleaner on the living room carpet, because she did not want to disturb her mother, that she realized how good she had come to feel in such a short time. But, in deciding not to vacuum, and perhaps disturb her resting mother, her attention was drawn back to the negative condition, and that dull, icky feeling came back into her stomach.

Wow! Sara pondered. *That's amazing. I can actually feel that the way I feel has only to do with what I am giving my attention to. The conditions did not change, but my attention did!*

Sara felt elated. She had discovered something very important. She had discovered that her joy is truly not dependent on anyone or anything else.

Then Sara heard her mother's bedroom door open, and her mother emerged from the hallway into the kitchen. "Oh, Sara, everything looks so nice!" her mother exclaimed, obviously feeling much better.

"Did your headache go away, Mom?" Sara asked, tenderly.

"It's much better now, Sara. I was able to rest for a while because I could tell you were out here taking care of things. Thank you, Sweetheart."

Sara felt wonderful. She knew that she had not actually *done* much more than she did every single day after school. Her mother was not appreciating Sara for her action. Her mother was appreciative of Sara's open valve. *I can do this,* Sara decided. *I can keep my valve open no matter the conditions.*

Sara remembered Solomon's affirmation: *I will keep my valve open — anyway!*

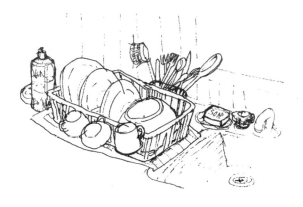

CHAPTER NINETEEN

Very nice, Sara — an A. Sara read the words scrawled across the top of yesterday's assignment, just handed back to her by Mr. Jorgensen.

Sara tried to stifle an ear-to-ear grin as she read the words written in bright red ink. Mr. Jorgensen glanced back at Sara as he handed the girl in front of Sara her paper, and when Sara's eyes met his, he winked at her.

Sara felt her heart jump. She felt very proud. This was a new feeling for Sara, and one, she noticed, that she liked very much.

Sara could not wait to get to the thicket to talk to Solomon.

"Solomon, what has happened to Mr. Jorgensen?" Sara asked. "He seems like a different man."

He's the same man, Sara, you're just noticing different things.

"I don't think I'm noticing different things, I think he's doing different things."

Like what, Sara?

"Well, like he smiles a lot more than he used to. And sometimes he whistles before the bell rings. He never used to do that. He even winked at me! And he's been telling better stories in class, making the class laugh more. Solomon, he just seems a whole lot happier than he used to."

Well, Sara. It sounds like your teacher may have joined your Chain-of-Joy.

Sara was stunned. Was Solomon actually trying to give Sara the credit for Mr. Jorgensen's change in behavior?

"Solomon, are you saying that I made Mr. Jorgensen happier?"

Well, it is not only your doing, Sara, because Mr. Jorgensen truly wants to be happy. But you did help him to remember that he wants to be happy. And you did help him to remember why he decided to become a teacher, to begin with.

"But Solomon, I haven't talked to Mr. Jorgensen about any of that. How could I have helped him to remember that?"

You did all of that, Sara, with your appreciation of Mr. Jorgensen. You see, any time you hold someone, or something, as your object of attention, and at the same time, you are feeling that wonderful feeling of appreciation — you add to their state of Well-being. You shower them with your appreciation.

"Like spraying them with the garden hose?" Sara giggled, pleased with her own silly analogy.

Yes, Sara. It is very much like that. But before you can actually spray them, you have to hook your hose to the faucet and turn it on. And that is what the appreciation does. Whenever you are feeling appreciation, or love, whenever you are seeing something positive about someone, or something, you are hooked to the faucet.

"Who puts the appreciation in the faucet, Solomon? Where does it come from?"

It has always been there, Sara. It is just naturally there.

"Well, then, why aren't more people spraying it around?"

Well, because most people have disconnected from the faucet, Sara. Not intentionally, but they just don't understand how to stay connected.

"Okay, then, Solomon, are you saying that I can hook up to it anytime that I want to and I can spray it around, anyplace, anytime, on anything I want to?"

That's right, Sara. And wherever you spray your hose of appreciation, you will begin to notice very obvious changes.

"Wow!" Sara whispered, mentally trying to size up the magnitude of what she had just learned. "Solomon, this is like magic!"

It seems like magic at first, Sara, but in time it begins to feel very natural. Feeling good — and then being a catalyst to help others feel good — is the most natural thing you will ever do!

Sara gathered her book bag and her discarded jacket, getting ready to tell Solomon good-bye for this day.

Just remember, Sara, your work is to stay hooked to the faucet.

Sara stopped and turned back to Solomon, realizing, suddenly, that this may not be as easy, or as magical, as Solomon had made it sound at first.

"Is there a trick to that, Solomon, to stay hooked to the faucet?"

It may take a little practice, at first. You'll get better and better at it. For the next few days, just think about something, and then pay attention to how you feel. You'll notice, Sara, that when you are appreciating, or basking, or applauding, or seeing positive aspects, you'll feel wonderful, and that means you're hooked to the faucet. But when you are blaming, or criticizing, or finding fault — you won't feel good. And that means you're unhooked, at least for the time you are feeling bad. Have fun with this, Sara. And with those last words, Solomon was gone.

Sara felt such exhilaration as she walked home that day. She had already enjoyed, very much, Solomon's game of appreciation, but the idea of appreciating with the intent of hooking to this wonderful faucet excited her even more. Somehow, it gave Sara more reason to appreciate.

Sara rounded the corner for the last stretch of her walk home and saw Old Aunt Zoie moving very slowly up her walkway. All winter long, Sara had not seen her at all, and she was surprised to see her outside. Aunt Zoie didn't see Sara, and so, Sara did not call out to her, not wanting to startle her, and, also, not wanting to get involved in the

long conversation that was probable. Aunt Zoie talked very slowly, and over the years, Sara had learned to avoid the frustration of seeing Aunt Zoic groping for words to express her thoughts. It was as if her mind worked so much faster than her mouth that she would get all mixed up about where she was within the thought. Sara's trying to help, by putting a word in here and there, only irritated Aunt Zoie. So Sara had decided that avoidance was the best solution. Although that never really felt right either. Sara felt sad as she watched this poor old woman hobbling up her stairs. She was holding onto the railing with all of her strength, taking one step at a time, very slowly moving up a set of four or five stairs onto her front porch.

I hope I'm not like that when I'm old. Sara thought. And then Sara remembered her last talk with Solomon. *The faucet! I'll shower her with the faucet! First, I connect to the faucet, and then I flow it all over her.* But the feeling wasn't there. *Okay, I'll try again.* Still, no feeling of being hooked up. Sara felt instant frustration. "But, Solomon," she pleaded, "this is really important. Aunt Zoie needs to be sprayed." No reply from Solomon. "Solomon, where are you?" Sara shouted out loud, not even realizing Aunt Zoie had now noticed her and was standing at the top of her stairs watching her.

"Who are you talking to?" Aunt Zoie barked.

Sara was startled and embarrassed. "Oh, nobody," she replied. And she scampered quickly down the path, past Aunt Zoie's garden, now just a muddy field waiting for the new spring planting. Red-faced and angry, Sara went home.

CHAPTER TWENTY

"Solomon, where were you yesterday?" Sara whined, as she encountered Solomon on his post. "I needed you to help me hook to the faucet so that I could help Aunt Zoie feel better."

Do you understand why you were having trouble hooking up, Sara?

"No, Solomon. Why couldn't I hook up? I really wanted to."

Why?

"I really wanted to help Aunt Zoie. She is so old and confused. Her life just can't be much fun."

And so, you wanted to hook to the flow, to shower Aunt Zoie, to fix what is wrong with her, so that she can be happy?

"Yes, Solomon. Will you help me?"

Well, Sara, I would like to help you, but I'm afraid that it is not possible.

"Why not, Solomon? What do you mean? She is really the nicest old lady. You'd like her, I think. I'm sure she has never done anything wrong..."

Sara, I am sure you are right. Aunt Zoie is a wonderful woman. The reason we can't help her, under these circumstances, has nothing to do with her; it's you, Sara.

"Me?! What did I do, Solomon? I'm just trying to help her!"

Yes, indeed, Sara. That is what you are wanting. It's just that you are going about it in a way that cannot work. Remember, Sara, your work is to connect to the faucet.

"I know that, Solomon. That's why I needed you. To help me hook up."

But you see, Sara, I can't help you, either. **You** *have to find that feeling place.*

"Solomon, I don't get it."

Remember, Sara, you cannot be part of the chain-of-pain and hooked to the faucet of Well-being at the same time. It's one or the other. When you are observing an unwanted condition which causes you to feel bad, that bad feeling is how you know that you are unhooked. And when you are not connected to the natural flow of Well-being, you have nothing to give to another.

"Good grief, Solomon, it seems impossible. If I see someone who needs help, just seeing them needing help makes me vibrate in a way that I can't help them. That's just awful. How can I ever help anybody?"

You have to remember that the most important thing is to stay connected to the faucet of Well-being. So, you must hold your thoughts in a position that keeps you feeling good. In other words, Sara, you have to be more aware of your connection to the faucet of Well-being than you are aware of the conditions. That's the key.

Sara, think back about what happened yesterday. Tell me what happened with Aunt Zoie.

"Okay. I was walking home from school, and I saw Aunt Zoie hobbling up her front sidewalk. She's all crippled up, Solomon. She can hardly walk at all. She has this old cane made out of real old wood that she uses to hold herself up."

And then what happened?

"Well, nothing really happened, I just was thinking how sad it is that she is so crippled..."

And then what happened?

"Well, nothing happened, Solomon..."

How were you feeling, about then, Sara?

"Well, Solomon, I felt real bad. I felt really sorry for Aunt Zoie. She could hardly pull herself up the steps. And then I felt scared that I might be like that when I get old, too."

Now that is the most important point in this whole thing, Sara. When you notice that you are feeling bad, that's how you know that you are looking at a condition that disconnects you from the faucet. You see, Sara, in truth, you are naturally hooked to the faucet. You don't have to work to get hooked to it. But it is important to pay attention to how you are feeling so you know when you are unhooked. That's what negative emotion is.

"But what should I have done to stay hooked up, Solomon?"

I have noticed, Sara, that when it is your top priority to stay hooked, you find more and more thoughts that keep you hooked up. But until you truly understand that that is what is most important, most of you will go off on all kinds of wild goose chases.

I will offer you a series of thoughts, or statements, and as you hear them, pay attention to the way you feel. Does the statement hook you up to the faucet or disconnect you from it?

"Okay."

Look at that poor, old woman. She can barely walk.

"Well, that feels bad, Solomon."

I just don't know what will happen to Aunt Zoie. She can barely get up the stairs now. What will she do when she gets worse?

"That unhooks me, Solomon. That's easy."

I wonder where her rotten children are. Why don't they come here and take care of her?

"I have wondered that, Solomon. And you're right. That unhooks me, too."

Aunt Zoie is a strong old woman. I think she likes her independence.

"Hmmm. That thought feels better."

Even if someone did try to take care of her, she probably wouldn't like that.

"Yes. That thought feels better, too. And that's probably true, Solomon. She gets mad at me when I try to do things for her." Sara remembered how impatient Aunt Zoie becomes when Sara impatiently tries to finish her sentences.

This wonderful old lady has lived a long, full life. I have no way of knowing that she is unhappy.

"That feels good."

She may very well be living exactly as she wants to live.

"That feels good, too."

I'll bet she has lots of great stories to tell of things she has seen. I'll stop and visit with her every now and again and find out.

"That feels very good, Solomon. I think Aunt Zoie would like that."

You see, Sara, you can look at the same subject, in this case the subject of Aunt Zoie, and find many different conditions to focus upon. And you can tell by the way you feel whether you are choosing a condition that is helpful or one that is not.

Sara felt so much better. "I think I am beginning to understand this, Solomon."

Yes, Sara, I believe you are. Now that you are consciously wanting to understand this, it is my expectation that you will have many opportunities to figure it out. Have fun with this, Sara.

CHAPTER TWENTY ONE

Things just seemed to be getting better and better. Every day seemed to have many more good things within it than bad things.

I am so glad that I have found Solomon. Or that Solomon has found me, Sara pondered, as she walked home from a day of school that had included not one negative incident. *Life really is getting better and better for me.*

Sara stopped at her leaning perch on the Main Street Bridge, and hanging way out over the swift moving river, she smiled broadly. Her heart was truly singing, and all was very well in Sara's world this day.

Hearing loud, boyish screeching, Sara looked up to see Jason and Billy running about as fast as she had ever seen them run. They were moving so fast, as they ran past her, she decided they must not have even noticed that she was perched there, and she watched them holding onto their hats and running at top speed past Hoyt's Store. Something about the way they were running made Sara laugh a little. They really did look sort of silly, running so fast that they had to hold their hats on. *Those two are always trying to break the sound barrier,* Sara smiled, but Sara noticed that they were not bothering her nearly as much as they used to. They hadn't changed, much, or really at all, but they were not getting under Sara's skin anymore. Not like before.

Sara waved at Mr. Matson, who, as usual, had his head under the hood of someone's car, and then picked up her pace as she headed toward Solomon's thicket. "What a beautiful day!" Sara spoke right out loud, looking upward into a beautiful blue-skied afternoon and breathing in the fresh spring air. Sara usually found her spirits rising once the last snow was melted and the spring grasses and flowers began. Winter was long, here. But it was not the passing of winter that cheered Sara so, but the passing of school. Three months of freedom, looming in the immediate future, was always reason for Sara to be glad. But somehow Sara knew that this happy heart was not about school nearing another year's end. This was about Sara's discovery of her valve. She had learned to keep it open — anyway.

It feels so good to feel free, Sara thought. *It feels so good to feel good. It feels so good not to be afraid of anything.....*

"EEEEKKKKKK!" Sara shrieked, as she found herself jumping high in the air to avoid walking right into the biggest snake she had ever seen, stretched out to its full length, which seemed endless, across the roadway. Coming down, well on the other side of it, Sara found herself running, at a dead run, one full country block, not slowing, in the least, until she was certain she had left that snake far behind.

"Well, maybe I'm not as fearless as I thought I was," Sara laughed to herself. And then she began to laugh even harder as she realized what had caused Jason's and Billy's burst of speed and lack of desire to stop and pester her. Sara was still laughing and panting as she walked into Solomon's thicket.

Solomon was waiting, expectantly and patiently, for Sara. *Well, Sara, you are filled with some new-found enthusiasm today?*

"Solomon, strange things are happening to me these days. Just when I think I really understand something, something else happens to make me realize I don't understand it at all. Just when I decide that I am truly brave, and afraid of nothing, something pops up that scares me to death. Things are very weird, Solomon."

You don't seem to be scared to death, Sara.

"Well, I exaggerated a bit, Solomon, because, as you can see, I am not dead..."

What I meant was, you don't appear to be frightened. You seem to be laughing, more than anything.

"Well, I am laughing now, Solomon, but I wasn't when that great big snake was lying in my path, just waiting to bite me. I had just been pointing out to myself how brave and fearless I am now, and then I felt instant fear and began running for my life."

Oh, I see. Solomon replied. *Sara, don't be too hard on yourself. It is perfectly normal to have a strong feeling response when you are faced with a condition that is not pleasing in some way. **It is not your initial response to something that sets the tone of your vibration — or of your point of attraction — it's what you do with it later that has lasting effect.***

"What do you mean?"

Why do you think the snake frightened you so, Sara?

"Because it's a snake, Solomon! Snakes are scary!

Snakes bite you, and make you sick. They can even kill you. Some of them wrap around you and break your ribs and smother you so you cannot breathe," Sara reported, proudly, remembering the details from the scary nature film she had seen at school.

Sara stopped to catch her breath and tried to settle down a little bit. Her eyes were flashing and her heart was pounding.

Sara, do you think that these words that you are offering here are making you feel better, or worse?

Sara had to stop and think for a moment because she was not even thinking about how her words were affecting her. She was just excited to explain how she felt about snakes.

You see, Sara, that's what I meant when I said that it is what you do next that is most important. As you are talking on and on about this snake and other snakes and all the bad things that snakes might do, you are holding yourself in that vibration — and it is becoming more and more likely that you will attract other uncomfortable experiences with snakes.

"But Solomon, what should I do? I mean, that big old snake was just lying there. And then I saw it. I almost stepped right on it. And then, no telling what it would have done to me..."

There you go again, Sara. You are still imagining — and holding as your image of thought — something that you do not want.

Sara was quiet. She knew what Solomon meant, but she didn't know what to do about it. The fact of the snake was sooooo big and sooooo close and sooooo scary she could not find another way to approach the subject. "Okay, Solomon, tell me what you would do if you were a little girl who almost stepped on a big snake."

Well, first of all, Sara, you have to remember that your goal is, first and foremost, to find a better feeling place. If you have any other goal, you will get very much off the track. If you try to figure out where all of the snakes are, you will feel worse. If you decide to be so alert that you never see another snake up close, you will feel overwhelmed. If you try to learn to identify all snakes, in order to label them good and bad, you will feel the impossible task of sorting all of that out. Sifting through the conditions will only make things worse. Your only goal is to try to approach this subject in a way that makes you feel better than you felt when you were jumping and running away from the snake.

"How would I do that, Solomon?"

You could say to yourself something like, "This big old snake is just lying there getting some sun. He is happy the winter is over, and the sun feels good to him, just like it feels good to me."

"I still don't feel better, though."

You could say something like, "This big old snake isn't the least bit interested in me. He didn't even look up as I ran by. He has many other things to do than bite little girls."

"Well, that does feel a little better. What else?"

"I sure am alert." Solomon continued. *"It is good that I saw the snake, or sensed it, and jumped over it so that I didn't bother it. The snake would do the same thing for me."*

"But would he, Solomon? How do you know that?"

Snakes live all around you, Sara. They are in the river. They are in the grasses where you walk. When you pass by, they get out of your way. They understand that there is enough room for everyone. They understand the perfect balance of your physical planet. They have their valves open, Sara.

"Snakes have valves?!"

They certainly do. All of the beasts of your planet have valves. And their valves are wide open most all of the time.

"Hmmmm," Sara pondered. She was feeling much better, now.

You see, Sara, how much better you feel? Nothing has changed. The snake is still lying right where you last saw him. The condition has not changed. But the way you feel certainly has changed.

Sara knew Solomon was right.

Sara, from now on when you think of snakes, you will feel positive emotion. Your valve will be open, their valve will be open. And you will continue to live in harmony.

Sara's eyes shined bright with her new understanding. "Okay, Solomon. I'd better go. I'll see you tomorrow."

Solomon smiled as Sara skipped down the path. Then Sara stopped and yelled back over her shoulder, "Solomon, do you think I'll ever be afraid of snakes again?"

Well, maybe, Sara. But if you are ever frightened, you know what to do about it.

"Yea," Sara grinned, "I do."

And eventually, Solomon added, *your fear will be completely gone. Not only about snakes, but about everything.*

As Sara walked home from the thicket, she looked off into the new spring grasses alongside the road and wondered how many snakes were hiding there. At first, she shivered a little at the frightening thought that snakes were hiding in the bushes along all of her private trails, but then she thought how nice they all had been to stay hidden and out of her way. How nice they had been not to jump out and scare her like Jason and Billy so often did. Sara smiled as she walked up her driveway and into her yard. She felt triumphant and strong. It felt good to leave fears behind. It felt really good.

CHAPTER TWENTY TWO

"Sara! Sara! Wow, Sara! Guess what? We found Solomon!"

Oh, no, that can't be! Sara thought, as she stood, frozen, on the street as Jason and Billy came speeding toward her on their bicycles.

"What do you mean, you found Solomon? Found him, where?"

"We found him over on Thacker's Trail, Sara. And guess what else?" Jason announced proudly. "We shot him!"

Sara felt so weak, she thought she would fall down. Her knees nearly buckled right out from under her.

"He was just sitting there on this post, Sara. So we flushed him up into the sky, and then Billy shot him with his BB gun. It was awesome, Sara! But he is not nearly as big as we thought he would be. He's mostly feathers."

Sara could not believe her ears. The impact of what she was hearing was so intense, so very important, and Jason was driveling on about Solomon not being as big as he thought he would be? Sara felt as if her head would explode. Her book bag dropped to the ground, and Sara began to run as fast as she had ever run in her life, to Solomon's thicket.

"Solomon! Solomon! Where are you, Solomon?!" Sara cried out, frantically.

Here, Sara, I'm here. Don't be alarmed.

And there, lying in a rumpled clump, was Solomon.

"Oh, Solomon," Sara cried, as she fell down on her knees in the snow. "Look at you! Look what they've done to you!"

Solomon was truly a mess. His always neat feathers were rumpled and seemed to be going in every direction, and the pure white snow all around Solomon was red with blood.

"Solomon, Solomon, what should I do?"

Sara, this is no big thing, really.

"But Solomon, you're bleeding. Look at all of this blood. Are you going to be all right?"

Of course, Sara. Everything is always all right.

"Oh, Solomon, please don't give me more of that 'All-Is-Well' junk. I can see, very well, with my own eyes, that All Is Not Well!"

Sara, come here to me, Solomon said.

Sara crawled right down next to Solomon and put her hand on his back and stroked the feathers under his chin. This was the first time that Sara had actually touched Solomon, and he felt so soft and so vulnerable. Tears rolled down Sara's cheeks.

Sara, don't get this rumpled pile of bones and feathers mixed up with who Solomon really is. This body is only a focal point — or a point of perspective — for something much more to see through. Your body is the same, Sara. It isn't really who you are. It is just the perspective that you use, for now, to allow who you really are to play and grow and rejoice.

"But, Solomon, I love you. Whatever will I do without you?"

Sara, wherever do you get this stuff? Solomon is not going anywhere. Solomon is forever!

"But, Solomon, you are dying!" Sara blurted, hurting more than she could ever remember hurting.

Sara, listen to me. I am not dying, because there is no such thing as death. True, I won't be using this body, for now, but it was getting old and a bit stiff, anyway. I've had a real crick in my neck ever since the day I tried to turn my head all the way around to please the Thacker's grandchildren.

Sara laughed through her tears. Solomon could nearly always make her laugh, even in the worst of times.

Sara, our friendship is forever. And that means that anytime you would like a chat with Solomon, all you have to do is identify what you are wanting to talk about, focus upon it, bring yourself to a place of feeling very good — and I'll be right here with you.

"But will I see you, Solomon? Will I be able to see you and touch you?"

Well, probably not, Sara. Not for a while, anyway, but Sara, that's not what our relationship is about, anyway.

We are mental friends, you and I.

And with those last words, Solomon's crumpled body relaxed into the snow, and his big eyes fluttered shut.

"No!!!!!" Sara's voice echoed across the pasture. "Solomon, don't leave me!"

But Solomon was quiet.

Sara stood up, looking down at Solomon's body. He looked so small, lying there in the snow, his feathers moving softly in the wind. Sara took off her coat and laid it on the snow next to Solomon. She lifted him, gently, onto her coat and wrapped it around him. And then, not noticing that it was really quite cold, Sara carried Solomon down Thacker's trail.

Sara, our friendship is forever. And that means that anytime you would like a chat with Solomon, all you have to do is identify what you are wanting to talk about and focus upon it, bring yourself to a place of feeling very good, and I'll be right here with you, Solomon said again — but Sara could not hear.

CHAPTER TWENTY THREE

Sara did not know what to do or where to begin to explain to her parents who Solomon was, or the important friend he had come to be to her. Her mind was spinning, and she was filled with regret that she had not told her family more about Solomon, because now she had no way to explain the tragedy that had befallen her. She had turned entirely to Solomon for guidance and comfort, and had all but severed those kinds of ties with her own family, and now she found herself faced with the loss of Solomon. She felt truly alone, with no place to turn.

She didn't know what to do with Solomon. The ground was still so frozen and hard, she knew she could not manage to dig a grave for him. The thought of tossing him into the coal furnace, in the furnace room, as she had seen her father do with dead birds or mice, was just too awful to even think about.

Sara was still sitting on the front steps of her house, holding Solomon in her arms, with tears flooding down her face, when her father's car skidded to a quick stop on the graveled driveway. He came rushing out of the car carrying Sara's wet book bag and crumpled pile of books. Sara had forgotten all about her things, left on the side of the road.

"Sara, Mr. Matson called me at work. He found your bag and books on the side of the road. We thought something had happened to you, Sara! Are you all right?"

Sara wiped at her wet face, embarrassed to have her father see her like this. She wanted to somehow hide Solomon, to continue to keep him a secret, and at the same time, she wanted, so much, to somehow find some comfort in telling her father everything.

"Sara, what has happened? What is wrong, Sweetheart?"

"Oh, Daddy," Sara blurted. "Jason and Billy have killed Solomon."

"Solomon?" her father questioned, as Sara opened her coat to let him see her dead friend.

"Oh, Sara, I'm so sorry." He had no idea why this dead owl was so significant to Sara, but it was clear that Sara was experiencing real trauma. He had never seen his daughter like this before. He wanted to take her in his arms and kiss her hurt away, but he knew that whatever had happened here was much too big for that. "Sara, give Solomon to me. I'll dig a grave for him behind the chicken coop. Go inside and get warm."

Only then did Sara realize how very cold she was. She reluctantly released her precious bundle and put Solomon in her father's arms. Sara felt weak, and so sad, and so very, very tired. She stayed seated on the steps as she watched her father gingerly carry her beautiful Solomon out of view. She smiled limply through her tears as she noticed how

seriously and delicately her father was carrying this feathered bundle, somehow seeming to understand how valuable
it was.

Sara flopped onto her bed, still fully clothed. She
kicked her shoes off onto the floor and sobbed into her pillow and then fell asleep.

CHAPTER TWENTY FOUR

Sara found herself standing in some strange thicket, surrounded by beautiful spring flowers, with bright col-
ored birds and butterflies flying all around her.

Well, Sara, it seems that you have much to talk about today,
Solomon quipped.

"Solomon!" Sara shouted with glee. "Solomon, you're
not dead, you're not dead! Oh Solomon, I'm so glad to see
you!"

Sara, why are you so surprised? I told you there is not death.

Now, Sara, what is it you are wanting to talk about?
Solomon offered, calmly, as if nothing at all out of the ordi-
nary had happened.

"Solomon, I know that you said that there is no such thing as death, but you looked dead. You felt limp, and heavy, and your eyes were shut, and you weren't breathing."

Well, Sara, you just became used to seeing Solomon in a certain way. But now you have an opportunity — because your wanting is so much greater than ever before — to see Solomon in a broader way. A more universal way.

"What do you mean?"

Well, most people see things only through their physical eyes, but you now have the opportunity to see things through broader eyes — more through the eyes of the True Sara that lives within the physical Sara.

"You mean there is another Sara living inside of me, like you are the Solomon who lives inside of my Solomon?"

Yes, Sara, that's it. And that Inner Sara lives on forever and ever. That Inner Sara will never die, just as this Inner Solomon, that you see here, will never die.

"Well, that sounds very good to me, Solomon. Will I see you back on Thacker's Trail tomorrow?"

No, Sara, I will not be there.

Sara, frowned.

But think about it, Sara! Whenever you wish to chat with Solomon, you may. No matter where you are. You don't have to walk to the thicket anymore. You have only to think of Solomon — and remember what it feels like to visit with Solomon — and I'll be right here to visit with you.

"Well, that sounds okay, Solomon. But I've loved our visits in the thicket. Are you sure you wouldn't just as soon go back there, like before?"

Sara, you'll come to like our new way of interacting even more than you have loved our fun in the thicket. There is no limitation in our new way of interacting. You'll see. We'll have great fun.

"Okay, Solomon. I believe you."

Good night, Sara.

"Solomon!" Sara cried out, not wanting Solomon to leave her so soon.

Yes, Sara?

"Thank you for not being dead."

Good night, Sara. All is well.

PART II

The Happily Forever Afterlife of Sara and Solomon

CHAPTER TWENTY FIVE

"Solomon, aren't you mad at Jason and Billy for shooting you?"

Why, Sara? Why would I want to be mad at them?

"Well, Solomon, they shot you!" Sara replied in amazement. How could Solomon not understand her question, and how could he not be mad at them for doing something so awful?

No, Sara. Whenever I think of Jason and Billy, I just appreciate them for bringing you to me.

"But, Solomon. Don't you think that shooting you is more significant than that?"

Sara, the only thing that is significant is that I feel good. And I cannot feel anger toward Jason and feel good at the same time. Keeping my valve open is most significant, Sara — so I always choose thoughts that feel good.

"Solomon, wait a minute. Are you saying that no matter how bad someone is, and no matter what sorts of awful things they do, you do not think about those things? That nobody ever does anything bad enough to make you mad at them?"

Sara, they all mean well.

"Oh, Solomon, come on. THEY SHOT YOU! How bad does it have to get before you understand how bad that is?"

Sara, let me ask you some questions. Do you think that if I got really, really mad at Jason and Billy for shooting me that they would stop shooting things?

Sara was quiet. She didn't think that Solomon's anger would make any difference. She had been angry at them countless times for shooting things, and it had never even slowed them down.

"No, Solomon. I guess not."

Can you think of any purpose that my anger would serve?

Sara thought about that, too.

If I became angry at them, it might make you feel more justified in your anger, Sara, but then I would only be joining your chain-of-pain, and no good could come from that.

"But, Solomon," Sara protested, "It just seems like..."

Sara, Solomon interrupted, *we could talk all day and all night about which actions are right and which actions are wrong. You could spend the rest of your lifetime trying to sort out which behaviors are appropriate and which are not, and under which conditions they are appropriate and under which conditions they are not appropriate. But what I have learned is that any time, even if it is one minute, that is spent trying to justify why I feel bad, is wasted life. And I have also learned that the faster I can get to a place of feeling good, the better my life is — and the more I have to offer to others.*

So, through lots of living and lots of experiencing, I have come to know that I can choose thoughts that close my valve or I can choose thoughts that open my valve — but in every case, it is MY choice. And so, I gave up on blaming the Jasons and Billys, long ago, because it didn't help me — and it didn't help them.

Sara was quiet. She was going to have to think about this one. She had already decided that she would NEVER forgive Jason for this terrible deed, and here Solomon was, unwilling to join her, even one little bit, in her blame.

Remember, Sara, if you let the conditions that surround you control the way you feel, you will always be trapped. But when you are able to control the way you feel — because you control the thoughts you offer — then you are truly liberated.

Sara remembered hearing something like that from Solomon, before, but then, nothing this big was challenging them. Somehow, this seemed too big to forgive.

Sara, in this big world where so many people have different ideas of what is right and wrong, you will often be faced with witnessing behavior that you may feel is inappropriate. Are you going to demand that all of those people change their ways, just to please you? Would you want to do that, even if you could?

The idea of everyone behaving in a way that would please her, did appeal to Sara in some ways, but she truly did not think that that was a likely thing. "Well, no, I guess not."

Then, what is the alternative? Will you hide yourself away, shielding yourself from witnessing their diverse behavior, making yourself a prisoner in this beautiful world?

Well, that option was really not to her liking, but Sara recognized remnants of that behavior in her not-so-distant past, as she often, mentally, had withdrawn from others, crawling into her own mind, keeping all, or most of them, outside. *Those were not happy times,* Sara remembered.

Sara, you will experience such joy when you are able to keep your valve open, anyway. When you are able to acknowledge that many people are choosing different things; they believe differently; they want differently; they act differently, and when you understand that all of that adds to a more perfect whole, and that none of that threatens you — because the only thing that affects you is what you are doing with your own valve — then you move about freely and joyously.

"But, Solomon, Jason and Billy did more than threaten you. They shot you. They killed you!"

Sara, you're still not over that, are you? Can you not see that I am not dead? Sara, I am very much alive. Did you think that I would want to live in that tired, old body of an owl, forever?

Sara knew that Solomon was teasing her, because he was neither tired-seeming, or old.

It is with great joy that I released that physical body, knowing that whenever I want to, I can pour my Energy into another, younger, stronger, faster.

"You mean, you wanted them to shoot you?"

It's co-creation, Sara. That's why I let them see me. So that they could co-create this very important experience. Not only for me, but for you, too, Sara.

Sara had been so overwhelmed with all that had happened since Solomon's shooting that she had not had time to wonder how it was that Jason and Billy were able to see Solomon.

The important thing to understand, Sara, is, first: all is truly well, no matter how it may seem to you from your physical perspective. And second, whenever your valve is open, only good things can come to you.

Sara, try to appreciate Jason and Billy as I do. You will feel much better.

"When pigs fly," Sara thought. And then she laughed at her own negative response. "I'll think about it, for you. But this is so different from anything I have ever thought about before. I have always been taught that when someone does something wrong, they should be punished."

The problem with that, Sara, is that all of you have a difficult time deciding who gets to decide what is wrong. Most of you believe that you are right, therefore, they must be wrong. Physical beings have been killing each other, for years, arguing about that one. And with wars and killings that have been taking place on your planet for thousands of years, you still have come to no agreement. You would all be much better off if you would just pay attention to your own valves. Life would be much better, right away.

"Do you think people will be able to learn about their valves? Do you think everyone will learn that?" Sara felt overwhelmed with the enormity of this endeavor.

*That does not matter, Sara. For the only thing that matters to you, is that **you** learn it.*

Well, that didn't seem so big. "Okay, Solomon, I'll work on this some more."

Good night, Sara. I have enjoyed our visit immensely.

"Me too, Solomon. Good night."

CHAPTER TWENTY SIX

Jason and Billy sped by Sara on their bicycles, calling out something obnoxious and inaudible. Sara smiled as they passed her by, and then she felt a little bit of surprise as she realized that they would disappoint her if they failed to be as bad as they could be, and that, in some strange way, the three of them were co-creators in this game they were always playing together. The game of, "I'm your rotten little brother, and this is my obnoxious, rotten little friend, and our task is to make your life miserable in every way we can, and your job is to respond to us in misery."

This is weird, Sara thought. *I'm not supposed to enjoy them. Whatever could be happening here?*

As Sara continued to walk toward home, out of habit she almost turned the corner to go to Solomon's thicket, forgetting, temporarily, that that was no longer their meeting place. That thought reminded Sara of Solomon's shooting, and that thought reminded Sara of Solomon's response to being shot by these two rotten little boys. And then, a very strong awareness came over Sara.

Jason and Billy shot Solomon, and Solomon still loves them. Solomon is able to keep his valve open even under those conditions, so maybe I'm learning to keep my valve open, too. Maybe my life is finally important enough to me that I am not bothered by what others are doing, or saying.

Goose bumps bumped up all over Sara's body. She felt light and tingly all over — and she knew that she had figured something out that was very significant.

That's good, Sara. I agree with you wholeheartedly, Sara heard Solomon's voice.

"Hi, Solomon. Where are you?" Sara asked, still longing for a visual Solomon to gaze upon as she chatted.

I'm here, Sara, Solomon replied, sliding past the question quickly, and getting on to more important business. *Sara, you have just stated the most important secret of life. You are coming to understand what unconditional love really is.*

"Unconditional love?"

Yes, Sara, you are coming to understand that you are a lover. You are a physical extension of pure, positive Nonphysical Energy, or love. And as you are able to allow that pure love Energy to flow, no matter what, in spite of the conditions that surround you — then you have achieved unconditional love. You are then, and only then, truly the extension of who you really are and who you have come here to be. You are then, and only then, truly fulfilling your purpose for being. Sara, this is very good.

Sara felt elated. She was not completely understanding the magnitude of what Solomon was saying, but she could tell, from the enthusiasm with which he was saying it, that it must be really important, and, she was certain that Solomon was very pleased with her.

Well, Sara, I know this sounds a bit strange to you in the beginning. It is a whole new orientation for most people, but until you understand this, you will never truly be happy. Not for long, anyway.

Sit here and just listen for a little while, and I'll explain to you how it all works.

Sara found a dry, sunny spot and plopped herself down to listen to Solomon. She loved listening to the sound of Solomon's voice.

There is a Stream of pure, positive Energy that flows to you at all times. Some may call it Life Force. It is called many different things, but it is the Stream of Energy that created your planet to begin with. And it is the Stream of Energy that continues to sustain your beautiful planet. This Stream of Energy keeps your planet spinning in its orbit in perfect proximity to other planets. This Stream maintains the perfect balance of your microbiology.

This Stream maintains the perfect balance of water on your planet. This is the Stream that keeps your heart pumping, even when you are asleep. This is a wonderful, powerful Stream of Well-being, Sara, and this Stream flows to each of you every minute of your day and night.

"Wow," Sara sighed, as she tried to understand this wonderful, powerful Stream.

As a person living on your planet, Sara, in any moment, you can allow or resist this wonderful Stream. You can let it flow to

you and through you, or you can disallow the Stream.

"Why would anyone not want this Stream?"

Oh, everyone would want it, Sara, if they understood it. And no one ever resists it on purpose. They just have habits that they have learned from each other that cause resistance to this Stream of

Well-being.

"Like what, Solomon?"

Well, Sara, the main thing that causes people to be resistant to the Stream of Well-being is their looking at the evidence that has been created by others who have been resistant to the Stream of Well-being.

Sara looked puzzled. She was not really getting this, yet.

You see, Sara, whenever you give your attention to anything, just by observing it you begin to vibrate as it is — while you are observing it. So if you are looking at sickness, for example, for the time you are looking at, or talking about, or thinking about sickness, you are not allowing the Stream of Well-being. You have to look at Well-being to allow Well-being.

Sara began to brighten. "Ah! This is like that birds of a feather stuff we talked about before. Isn't it?"

That's right, Sara. It's about Law of Attraction. If you want to attract wellness, you must vibrate with wellness. But if you give your attention to someone who is sick, you cannot allow wellness at the same time.

Sara began to pucker as she thought about what Solomon was saying. "But, Solomon, I thought I was supposed to help people who are sick. And how can I help them if I don't look at them?"

It's okay to look at them, Sara, but don't see them as sick. See them as getting better. Better yet, see them as well, or remember them when they were well. That way, you don't use them as your reason to stop the Stream from flowing to you.

It is not easy for people to hear this, Sara, because they are so conditioned to observing everything around them. If they only knew, that when they look at things that make them feel negative emotion, that that feeling is their signal that they have just disallowed the Stream of Well-being, I do not think so many people would be so willing to look at so many things that make them feel bad.

Sara, just for a moment, here, don't try to understand what most others are doing. Just listen to this. There is one constant, steady Stream of Well-being, and it is flowing to you at all times. When you feel good, you are allowing the Stream, and when you feel bad, you are not allowing the Stream. Now, when you understand that, what is it that you want most to do?

"Well, I want to feel good as much as I can."

Good. Now, let's say you are watching television, and you see something that makes you feel bad.

"Yea, like when somebody gets shot, or killed, or hurt in an accident?"

Yes, like that. When you see that, Sara, and you feel bad, do you understand what is happening?

Sara smiled brightly. "Yes, Solomon, I am resisting the Stream."

You've got it, Sara! Whenever you are feeling bad, you are resisting the Stream. Whenever you are saying NO, you are pushing against, and therefore resisting the Stream.

Sara, when someone says NO to cancer, they are actually disallowing the Stream of Well-being. When someone says NO to murderers, they are actually disallowing the Stream of Well-being. When someone says NO to poverty, they are actually resisting the Stream of Well-being — because when you are giving your atten-

tion to what you don't want, you are vibrating with it, which means you are resistant to what you do want. So, the key is to identify what you don't want, briefly, but then to turn to what you DO want and say, YES.

"That's it?! That's all we have to do? Just say YES instead of NO!" Sara could not believe how simple this all sounded. She felt elated. "Solomon, that is so easy! I can do that! I think everybody could do that!"

Solomon enjoyed Sara's enthusiasm for this new knowledge. *Yes, Sara, you can do that. And that is what you have come forth to teach to others. Practice it for a few days. Pay attention to yourself and others around you, and notice how practiced most of you are at saying NO to things much more often than you say YES to things. As you observe, for a while, you will come to understand the sorts of things that people do to resist the Wellbeing that is natural. Have fun with this, Sara.*

CHAPTER TWENTY SEVEN

All the next day, Sara's thoughts kept drifting back to what she and Solomon had last talked about. Sara was truly excited about coming to understand something which Solomon seemed to think was so very important, but the more time that elapsed since her conversation with Solomon, the more she wasn't sure, at all, that she had understood what Solomon was trying to teach her. Sara did remember, though, that Solomon encouraged her to observe others, to see how much more often they said NO than YES, and so, Sara decided to pay close attention to that.

"Sara, I don't want you to be late tonight," her mother warned. "We are having company for dinner, and I'll need you. We don't want our company to visit us in a messy house, now do we?"

"Okay," Sara sighed, reluctantly. Company was not her favorite thing. Not even close to her favorite thing.

"Now, Sara, I mean it. Don't be late!"

Sara stopped in the doorway, happily surprised to have found some evidence, so early in the morning, that supported what Solomon had said. She moved slowly, sort of staring off into the distance as she reviewed what she could remember of Solomon's words, unknowingly letting cold air fill the living room as she stood in the open doorway.

"Sara! Don't stand there letting cold air in! For heavens sake, Sara, get going. You're going to be late for school."

Wow! Sara mused. It was amazing. Her mother had just, in the last two minutes, offered five clear statements of what she did not want, and Sara could not remember even one statement about what her mother did want. And the amazing thing was, her mother didn't even notice what she was doing.

Sara's father was just finishing pushing snow from the front sidewalk when Sara skipped down the front steps. "Be careful, Sara. The walkway is slippery. You don't want to fall."

Sara grinned from ear to ear. *Wow,* she thought. *This is amazing!*

"Sara, did you hear me? I said, watch out, or you will fall down."

Sara didn't actually hear her father saying NO to anything, but his words certainly were pointed at what he did not want.

Sara's mind was spinning. She wanted to speak what she did want. "I'm okay, Daddy," she said. "I never fall down." *Whoops,* Sara thought. *That wasn't exactly saying YES.*

Wanting to be the best example that she could be for her father, Sara stopped and turned directly to her father and said, "Thank you, Daddy, for keeping the walkway clear for us. It makes it easy for me to not fall down."

Sara laughed right out loud as she heard herself, even when she was deliberately trying to say YES, still talking about not falling down. *Boy,* Sara thought, *this is not going to be easy.* And then again she laughed and then said right out loud, in amazement at herself, "NOT GOING TO BE EASY? Good grief, Solomon, I see what you mean."

Sara was only about 200 yards from her driveway when she heard the front door of her house slam shut, and she turned to see Jason running at top speed, holding his book bag in one hand and holding his hat on with the other hand, fast approaching Sara. Sara could see, from the fast approach Jason was making, and from the gleam she recognized in his eyes, that he was about to brush Sara from behind, as he had done dozens of times before, just enough to set her off balance and to make her mad. And, in anticipation, Sara shouted, "Jason don't you dare...... Jason, NO, darn you, Jason, don't doooooo that!" Sara shouted with all her might.

Good grief, Sara thought. *I'm doing it again. NO just keeps coming out of me, even when I don't want it to. Don't want it to?*

There I go again. Sara felt almost frantic. She could not seem to control her own words.

Jason brushed past Sara and kept on running, and as he was now over a block ahead of her, Sara began to relax into her own quiet walk to school and to reflect on the amazing events that she had observed over the past ten minutes.

Sara had decided to make a list of the NOs that she had heard so that she could sort it out later with Solomon. Taking her little notebook from her book bag, Sara wrote:

DON'T BE LATE.

DON'T WANT A MESSY HOUSE.

DON'T LET COLD AIR IN.

DON'T BE LATE FOR SCHOOL.

DON'T WANT TO FALL DOWN.

NOT GOING TO BE EASY.

JASON, DON'T YOU DARE.

Sara heard Mr. Jorgensen shouting at two boys in her classroom, "Don't run in the hallway!" Sara wrote it in her book. She was leaning up against her locker when another teacher from another classroom walked past her and said, "Hurry up, you're going to be late." Sara wrote that down, too.

Sara sat in her seat, trying to settle into another long day in school, when she saw the most amazing sign posted at the front of the classroom. The sign had been there all of this school year, but Sara had not noticed it before. Not like she was noticing it now. She could barely believe her eyes. She took out her notebook and began writing what she was reading:

NO TALKING IN CLASS.

NO GUM CHEWING.

NO FOOD OR DRINK IN THE CLASSROOM.

NO TOYS ALLOWED.

NO SNOW BOOTS IN THE CLASSROOM.

NO STARING OUT THE WINDOW.

NO LATE WORK PERMITTED.

NO PETS ALLOWED IN THE CLASSROOM.

TARDINESS NOT PERMITTED.

Sara sat stunned. *Solomon is right. Most of us do resist our Well-being.*

Sara was eager to hear and observe as much as she could that day. During lunch time, she sat off by herself away from the other kids, listening to the conversation two teachers were having at the table behind her. She could not see them, but she could clearly hear them.

"Oh, I don't know," one teacher said. "What do you think?"

"Well, I wouldn't do it if I were you." The other teacher replied. "You never know. You could end up much worse off than you are now."

Wow, Sara thought. She had no idea what they were talking about, but one thing was absolutely clear. The advice was NO, to whatever it was.

Sara added to her list:

I DON'T KNOW.

I WOULDN'T DO IT IF I WERE YOU.

Sara was not half way through this school day, and she already had two pages of NOs to discuss with Solomon.

Sara's afternoon proved as fruitful as her morning as she added to her list:

DON'T THROW THAT!

STOP THAT!

I SAID NO!

CAN YOU NOT HEAR ME?!

AM I NOT MAKING MYSELF CLEAR?

NO PUSHING!

I'M NOT GOING TO TELL YOU AGAIN!

By the end of the day, Sara was absolutely exhausted. It seemed to Sara that the whole world was resisting its Well-being.

"Boy, Solomon, are you ever right. Most everybody is saying NO instead of YES. Even me, Solomon. I know what I am supposed to do, and I can't even do it."

"I CAN'T DO IT." Sara wrote on her list.

What a day this had been.

That's quite a list you have there, Sara. You've had a busy day.

"Oh, Solomon, you don't know the half of it. This is only some of what I heard today. People are mostly saying NO, Solomon. And they don't even know it! And me too, Solomon. This is hard."

Well, Sara, it really isn't so hard once you know what to look for and once you realize what your goal is. Sara, read something to me from your list, and I'll show you what I mean.

"DON'T BE LATE."

Be on time.

"DON'T WANT COMPANY TO VISIT A MESSY HOUSE."

We want our home to be comfortable for our guests.

"DON'T LET COLD AIR IN."

Let's keep our house nice and warm.

"DON'T BE LATE FOR SCHOOL."

Being on time really feels best.

"DON'T WANT TO FALL DOWN."

Stay focused and coordinated.

"NOT GOING TO BE EASY."

I'll figure this out.

"DON'T RUN IN THE HALLWAY."

Be considerate of others.

"NO TALKING IN CLASS."

Let's discuss and learn together.

"NO STARING OUT THE WINDOW."

Your full attention will be of tremendous benefit to you.

"NO LATE WORK PERMITTED."

Let's stay current and work together.

"NO PETS ALLOWED IN THE CLASSROOM."

Your pets are much happier at home.

"Gosh, Solomon, you are really good at this."

*Sara, you'll be good at it, too. It just takes practice. And, Sara, the words that you use are not so very important. It's the feeling of **pushing against** that is detrimental. When your mother said, "Don't leave the door open," she was certainly **pushing against** what she did not want. But even if she had said, "Close the door!" she was still more aware of what she did not want, and therefore, still, her vibration would have been one of* pushing against.

I am wanting you to get the idea of relaxing toward what you do want, rather than pushing against what you do not want.

Certainly, your words are an indicator of your direction, but the way you feel is even a more clear indicator of your allowing or resisting.

Just have fun with this, Sara. **When you push against saying NO, you are still pushing against.** *The idea is just to talk more and more about what you DO want.* *And as you do that, things will just get better and better.* *You'll see.*

CHAPTER TWENTY EIGHT

Sara walked home, on this the last day of school for this year, with a strange mix of feelings. Usually, this was the happiest time of her year, having a full summer of near solitude ahead of her, not being forced to mix with a room full of different, and often uncomfortable, classmates. But on this year, the last day felt different to Sara. She had changed so very much in this very short year.

Sara walked briskly, breathing in the wonderful spring air, looking ahead, and then walking backwards for awhile. She was eager to see everything and everyone around her. The sky was more beautiful than she ever remembered seeing it. Bluer. Deeper in color. And the fluffy white clouds, in such stark contrast, were absolutely stunning. Sara could hear the sweet, clear songs of birds that were far enough away she could not see them, but their perfect songs were reaching her ears, anyway. The feel of the wonderful air upon her skin was truly delicious. Sara was walking in a state of true ecstacy.

So you see, Sara, WELL-BEING truly does abound.

"Solomon, it's you!"

It is everywhere. Solomon's clear words continued in Sara's head.

"It **is** everywhere, Solomon. I can see it, and feel it!"

In fact, it is everywhere that it is not disallowed. A constant, steady Stream of Well-being flows to you at all times, and, in any moment, you are allowing it or resisting it. And you are the only one that can allow or resist this constant, steady Stream of Well-being.

In all of the time that we have been visiting, the most important thing that I have wanted you to learn is the process of reducing, or eliminating, the patterns of resistance that you have learned from other physical people. Because, if it was not for the resistance that you have picked up along this physical trail, the Well-being that is natural to you, certainly the Well-being that you deserve, would flow, naturally, to you. To all of you.

Sara thought back about all of the wonderful conversations she had had with Solomon. How wonderful their interactions had been! And Sara realized that in every case, with every single conversation they had experienced together, Solomon had been helping Sara to lower resitance.

She thought back on the techniques, or games, Solomon had offered day after day, and now, from her clearer perspective, she realized that, all along, Solomon had been teaching her processes to lower resistance.

Little by little, Sara had learned to leave her resistance behind.

You, too, are a teacher, Sara.

Sara's eyes widened, and she felt breathless, as her favorite teacher of all time announced that she, like Solomon, was a teacher. Sara felt that warm feeling of appreciation sweep through her and around her.

And what you have come to teach, Sara, is that all really is well. Through the clarity of your example, many others will come to understand that there truly is nothing to push against. And that, in fact, the pushing against is the reason for not allowing the Well-being.

Sara could feel a special intensity about Solomon's words. His words were thrilling Sara. She didn't know what to say.

She walked up her graveled driveway and into her front yard feeling so wonderful she wanted to leap into the air. Then she bounded up the front steps and into the house. "Hi, I'm home!" Sara called, to anyone who might be inside.

CHAPTER TWENTY NINE

Sara went to bed early, eager to get back to her conversation with Solomon. She closed her eyes and breathed deeply as she tried to find that wonderful place where she and Solomon had left off. "All really is well," Sara said, aloud, with a calm, clear voice of absolute knowing. And then she opened her eyes in amazement.

Solomon, who Sara had not seen in weeks, was now hovering just above her bed. But his wings were not moving at all. It was as if he was suspended in air, effortlessly, hanging just above Sara's head. "Solomon!" Sara shouted in glee. "I am sooooo glad to see you!"

Solomon smiled and nodded.

"Solomon, you are so beautiful!"

Solomon's feathers were snow white and glowed as if each were a tiny spotlight. He seemed so much bigger and so much brighter but it was Sara's Solomon, all right. She could tell that by looking deep into his eyes.

Come fly with me, Sara! There is so much I want you to see!

And even before Sara could speak her agreement, she felt that incredible whoosh that she had felt before, when she had flown with Solomon, and they were off, but this time they were high above her little town. In fact, they were so high above her town, she did not recognize anything that she saw.

Sara's senses were dramatically heightened. Everything she saw was amazingly beautiful. Colors were deeper and more wonderful than she had ever seen. The smell in the air was intoxicating; never had Sara beheld such wonderful fragrances. Sara could hear beautiful sounds of birds singing and water flowing and wind whistling. Sounds of wind chimes and happy children's voices were wafting around her. The feel of the air on her skin was soothing and comforting and exciting. Everything looked and smelled and sounded and felt delicious.

"Solomon," she said, "it is all so beautiful!"

Sara, I want you to know the utter Well-being of your planet.

Sara could not imagine what Solomon had in store for her, but she was ready and willing to go anywhere he wanted her to go. "I'm ready!" Sara exclaimed.

And in a flash, Sara and Solomon flew far from planet Earth, out, out, out beyond the moon, beyond the planets, and even beyond the stars. In an instant, they had traveled, what must have been light years, to where Sara could see her beautiful planet turning and glistening far off in the distance, moving in a sort of perfect rhythm with the moon and other planets and stars and the Sun.

As Sara looked at the planet Earth, a feeling of total Well-being filled her little body. She watched with a sense of pride as the Earth turned steadily and certainly on its axis, as if it were dancing with other partners, all of whom knew exactly their part in the magnificent dance.

Sara gasped in amazement.

Look at it, Sara. And know that all is well.

Sara smiled and felt that warm wind of appreciation envelop her.

The same Energy that created your planet, to begin with, still flows to your planet to sustain it. A neverending flow of pure, positive Energy is flowing to all of you at all times.

Sara looked at her planet with complete knowing that this was true.

Let's take a closer look, now, Solomon said.

Now, Sara could not see any of the other planets, but planet Earth was glowing radiantly within her full view.

She could clearly see the dramatic definition between the land and the seas. The shorelines looked as if they had been emphasized with a giant marking pen, and the water shimmered as if there were millions of lights beneath the water, lighting the seas just for her viewing from her heavenly perspective.

Do you know, Sara, that the water that has been nurturing your planet for millions of years is the same water that nurtures your planet today? That is Well-being, Sara, of immense proportion.

Think about it, Sara. Nothing new is being trucked or flown into your planet. The immeasurable resources that exist, continue to be rediscovered by generation after generation. The potential for glorious life remains constant. And physical beings discover, to varying degrees, that perfection.

Let's look closer.

Solomon and Sara swooped down over the sea, and Sara could smell the wonderful sea air, and she knew that all is well. They soared faster than the wind over the great Grand Canyon, a large, long, jagged crack in the Earth's crust.

"What is that?!" Sara gasped in amazement.

That is evidence of your Earth's constant ability to keep its balance. Your Earth is continually seeking balance. That is evidence of that.

Now, flying round the Earth at about the same distance from the Earth that the airliners fly, Sara enjoyed the incredible landscape below. So much green, so much beauty, so much Well-being.

"What is that?" Sara questioned, pointing at the little cone protruding from the surface of the Earth and puffing big clouds of gray and black smoke.

That's a volcano, Solomon replied. *Let's get a closer look.* And before Sara could protest, off they went, diving down closer to the Earth, flying right through the smoke and dust.

"Wow!" Sara shouted. She was amazed at her feeling of absolute Well-being even though the smoke was so dense she could not see one thing in front of her. They flew up and out of the smoke, and Sara looked down to see this amazing volcano spitting and spewing.

That is more evidence of Well-being, Sara. It is another sign that your Earth is managing to keep its perfect balance.

And then they flew, up, up, up, again, and off to another amazing sight. It was a fire. A very big fire. Sara could see what looked like miles of red and yellow flames, hidden at times by big clouds of smoke. The wind was blowing very hard, and the smoke would sometimes clear, leaving a very good view of the flames, and then get so dense, Sara couldn't see the flames at all for a while. Every now and again, Sara would get a glimpse of an animal running very fast away from the fire, and she felt very sad that the fire was destroying the beautiful forest and the homes of so many animals.

"Oh, Solomon, that is just awful," Sara whispered, responding to the conditions she was witnessing.

That is only more evidence of Well-being, Sara. It is more evidence of your Earth seeking its balance. If we could stay here long enough, you would see how the fire will add much needed nutrition to the soil. You would see new seeds germinating and thriving, and in time, you would see the amazing value of this fire, which is part of the over-all balance of your planet.

"I'm just sad for the animals who are losing their homes, I guess."

Don't be sad for them, Sara. They are guided to new homes. They feel no lack. They are extensions of pure, positive Energy.

"But some of them will die, Solomon," Sara protested.

Solomon just smiled, and then, Sara smiled, too.

It's hard to get over that "death thing," isn't it? All is very well here, Sara. Let's explore some more.

Sara loved the feeling of Well-being that was enveloping her. She had always thought of the sea as treacherous, with sharks and shipwrecks. The television reports that she had seen of volcanoes spewing had always frightened her The news was always full of forest fires and disasters, and Sara realized, now, that she had been pushing hard against all of them.

This new point of view felt ever so much better. These things, that Sara had always assumed were terrible, or tragedies, now took on entirely new meaning when seen through the new eyes that Solomon had given her.

Sara and Solomon flew all night long, stopping to observe the amazing Well-being of Sara's planet. They saw a baby calf being born and baby chickens kicking their way out of eggs. They saw thousands of people driving in cars, and only a few of them bumping into each other. They saw thousands of birds moving to warmer climates and some farm animals growing longer hair for the winter. They saw gardens being harvested and other gardens being planted. They saw new lakes forming and new deserts forming. They saw people and animals being born, and they saw people and animals dying — and in every bit of every bit of all of it, Sara knew that all really was well.

"Solomon, how ever will I ever explain this to anybody? How will I ever make them understand?"

Sara, that is not your work. It is enough, Sweet Girl, that you understand.

Sara sighed a big sigh of relief, and then she felt her mother shaking her, "Sara, get up! We have lots to do." Sara opened her eyes to find her mother bending over her, and as she emerged into wakefulness, she pulled the covers over her head, wanting to hide from this day.

All truly is well, Sara. Sara heard Solomon's words. *Remember our journey.*

Sara pulled the blankets down from her head and smiled the most beautiful smile at her mother.

"Thanks, Mom!" Sara said. "I'll be fast as the wind. It'll be all right. You'll see. I'll be ready in a flash."

Her Mother stood stunned as she watched Sara bound from her bed, moving with deftness and clarity, and, most obviously, in joy.

Sara threw open her curtains and raised up her window and stretched out her arms with a big smile on her face. "What a beautiful day!" she exclaimed, with such enthusiasm that her mother stood bewildered, scratching her head.

"Sara, are you all right, Sweetheart?"

"I am perfect!," Sara said clearly. "All truly is well!"

"Well, if you say so, Honey," Sara's mother said, tentatively.

"And I do," Sara said, rushing in to the bathroom and smiling from ear to ear. "I do say so!"

THE END

SARA. BOOK 2 — Sara and Seth, Solomon's Fine Featherless Friends

...My family had read the first Sara book and were captivated by its wisdom and clarity. I knew we were in for a treat with this new story, "Sara and Seth", but I had no idea just how much of an impact it would have on all of us.

The sheer brilliance of this unassuming little book with its powerful message (of Well-Being) will leave you breathless.

(all ages)

— by Denise Tarsitano in the "Rising Star Series."

THE BOOK

When Seth moves into Sara's mountain town, and right into the middle of all of the secrets of Thacker's Trail, Sara doesn't know what to do with him. She is drawn to him in a strange and powerful way, but the idea of letting anyone in on her unbelievable secrets seems impossible. But Sara soon comes to trust Seth, and together they embark on an even more wonderful experience with Solomon.

Seth has been gathering important questions all of his very short life. He can barely believe his good fortune in meeting Solomon, who understands all things.

You'll enjoy seeing Sara's good life getting even better, and Seth's rather awful life becoming wonderful. And like everyone else, you will love Solomon.

BOOK: Ask for SARA-2 — $15 (plus S/H) Softcover ISBN# 0-9621219-7-5

THE TAPES

Sara and Seth, Solomon's Fine Featherless Friends is now available as an unabridged book on tape. Containing three audio-cassettes, this album offers over four hours of inspiring, uplifting and adventurous listening.

Relaxing with closed eyes, you can now comfortably absorb the pleasure of this extraordinary magical relationship between Sara and her new friend of a feather, Seth... plus, her ethereal owl friend, Solomon, makes his welcome reappearance, adding his wise perspective to their/our learning experiences.

CASSETTES: Ask for S3S2 — $30
(830) 755-2299 (Order form page C24)

SARA: BOOK 3
A Talking Owl is Worth a Thousand Words

...Add me to the list! The list of those that were totally delighted, enchanted, and inspired by your newest book, *Sara 3*. I read it in two sittings. I read it out loud as if I had an audience of eager listeners hanging onto every word. A few times I had to stop, lift my glasses and wipe away the tears. I have never enjoyed reading a book as much as I did this book. (all ages)

by Kathy Johnson—NC

THE BOOK

Sara has a hard time understanding why Seth wants to befriend the new girl in town and even share their secrets of Thacker's Trail. Even Solomon's reassuring words don't soothe Sara. But Sara discovers that not only does Annette's presence not detract from her joyful experience, but that it adds to it in many more ways than she could have imagined. The secrets of Thacker's Trail are known by more than Sara knew, and it turns out that Sara doesn't mind sharing her secrets as much as she at first believed.

Life just gets better and better for these extraordinary young people. And yours will, too, as you read their stories.

BOOK: Ask for SARA-3 — $15 (plus S/H) Softcover ISBN# 0-9621219-9-1

THE TAPES or CD's

Sara 3: A Talking Owl Is Worth a Thousand Words, is now available as an unabridged book on tape. Containing three audio-cassettes, this album offers over four hours of inspiring, uplifting and adventurous listening.

Sara's adventures expand as she and her best friend, Seth, are joined by Annette, a new girl in school.

Let Jerry's expressive voice transport you to Sara's world. A world of fun, and learning—and such good feelings.

Ask for S3S3 — Cassettes—$30; CD's—$45
(830) 755-2299 (Order form page C24)

The Science of Deliberate Creation

A Quarterly Journal and Catalog Addendum

Oct, Nov, Dec, 1999 — VOL 10

A Simple Choice: Which Thought Feels Better?

Newest Group Series — Spring, 1999 Album

Newest Book! Sara & Seth... and Solomon

Quarterly Quotes

A s you choose thoughts that feel better on day one, on day two, you will have access to a whole different set of choices — because each day you will have re-established your Vibrational Tone to your pure, positive Source Energy.   Phoenix, AZ — G-3/21/99

Abraham-Hicks Publications
P.O. Box 690070, San Antonio, TX 78269
Tel. (830) 755-2299 or FAX (830) 755-4179
On line — www.abraham-hicks.com
© Copyright 1999

Well, we did it! We picked up our new American Eagle motor coach on August 31st. Jerry's plan is to get within 200 miles of 95% of the population of the US, and this will allow us to hold seminars in 57 cities in the year 2000. Are we having fun, or what?!

As they heard Abraham discussing our new motor coach and the fun we are having adapting to this new way of living, our dear friends from phenomeNEWS whispered to each other, "They are playing house." Is that why we are having sooooooooo much fun?

We've been trying to pinpoint exactly what is at the root of our extraordinary, outrageous joy.

Is it the fun of meeting a constant stream of new happy people out looking for a wonderful adventure in this day? It may be that.

Is it the feeling of appreciation that we feel at the constant stream of other coach owners who have been so kind and so eager to share with us their knowledge about how to successfully operate our new coach? It may be that.

Or is it spending each day in a beautiful place filled with new promise to surprise and delight us. Walking through beautiful wooded parks, smelling campfires and dinners cooking, hearing happy children and adults all around? Might be that.

Is it the feeling of appreciation and pride that we feel for our efficient, effective staff back in Texas who tend to everything while we are away? Might be that.

Is it the feeling of triumph of taking in such a pile of new technical information and then actually applying it to make this Monster Bus actually work for us? That could be it.

Or is it the thrill of floating down the highway on the cushion of air that has been built into this contraption with a wide angle view out the front window unlike anything we've experienced before? That could be it.

Is it graham crackers and milk in the middle of the night? That's probably it.

Is it the feeling of exhilaration that comes from discovering yet another great way to do something: like Jerry's great idea of building a desk that magically appears beneath our rear bed when the hydraulic lifts raise the bed up to accomodate my Mac computer and printer? It always feels like the Bat Mobile emerging from the Bat Cave. I'll bet that's it.

Or is the fun we are having with other big rigs, truckers, Rv'ers, and the like who smile as they pass, or wave, or, my personal favorite, blink their courtesy lights to say come on in the lane is clear? I blink our courtesy lights a lot. That could be it.

Is it the feeling of success at putting to rest unwarranted fears such as, "Are we too tall to go under that bridge?" or "Are we too wide to go through that toll booth?" or "Are we to big to squeeze between those trees?" For it really is sweet relief to let fears fall away and return to our state of knowing that All Truly Is Well, no matter what. Might be that.

Is it the necessity for better Segment Intending, since the different aspects of our day are truly specific segments. Even starting the engine requires concentration. The diesel engine wants more specific attention than any other vehicle we have driven. Putting the leveling jacks up or down is a specific process with a clearly defined order. Hooking the tow car to the bus and disengaging the drive shaft, making sure the gear level is in the proper position and that the brake is not on, all require attention that we have discovered feels wonderful to give.

Certainly is it all of this and much much more, but the thing that we are more aware of than anything else is that we are living what Abraham has been teaching us for years. That the more decisions we make in any day the better we will feel — because in each decision there is a focusing of Energy. And that Energy is Life Force. Never before have we felt so focused or so eager or so alive.

We are continually appreciative of our spectacular lives. We love coming to see all of you in your beautiful cities across this nation. And we love more than we are ever able to express in words your magnificent questions and beautiful faces and willingness to draw from Abraham more and more clarity about how all of this works.

We want everyone who desires it to feel joy as we have found it.

We love you very much, and we'll see you along the way.

And if you see a big beautiful, mostly white with silver swirls, 40 foot American Eagle motor coach with a silver Chevy Tahoe in tow, floating down the highway with two smiling people blinking their courtesy lights at you — that would be us, living happily ever after.

Our love, *Jerry + Esther*

90 DAY EVENT SCHEDULE DETAILS

From time to time there are changes in our scheduling, so please reserve in advance with our San Antonio office at (830) 755-2299.

PREPAID RESERVATIONS ARE REQUIRED.

If you cancel 7 days, or less, before any event, a $50 cancellation fee will be charged.

11/1/03 — Dallas, TX — Held at the Dallas Marriott Quorum, 14901 Dallas Parkway, Dallas, TX 75254. (972) 661-2800. Saturday 9AM to 4:20PM. $150.00.

11/22/03 — San Antonio, TX — Held at the Abraham-Hicks Facility, 28550 Old Fredericksburg Rd., Fair Oaks, TX 78015. (830) 755-2299. Saturday 9AM to 4:20PM. $150.00.

12/6/03 — Tampa, FL — Held at the Tampa Marriott Westshore, 1001 N. Westshore Blvd., Tampa, FL 33607. (813) 287-2555. Saturday 9AM to 4:20PM. $150.00.

12/13/03 — Boca Raton, FL — Held at the Renaissance Boca Raton, 2000 NW 19th St., Boca Raton, FL 33431. (561) 368-5252. Saturday 9AM to 4:20PM. $150.00.

12/20/03 — Orlando, FL — Held at the Embassy Suites, Lake Buena Vista Resort, 8100 Lake Ave., Orlando, FL 32836. (407) 239-1144. Saturday 9AM to 4:20PM. $150.00.

1/24/04 — San Antonio, TX — Held at the Abraham-Hicks Facility, 28550 Old Fredericksburg Rd., Fair Oaks, TX 78015. (830) 755-2299. Saturday 9AM to 4:20PM. $150.00.

1/31/04 — West Los Angeles, CA — Held at the Courtyard Marriott, 13480 Maxella Ave., Marina del Rey, CA 90292. (310) 822-8555. Saturday 9AM to 4:20PM. $150.00.

2/7/04 — San Diego, CA — Held at Embassy Suites, 4550 La Jolla Village Dr., San Diego, CA 92122. (858) 453-0400. Saturday 9AM to 4:20PM. $150.00.

2/21/04 — San Rafael, CA — Held at the Four Points Sheraton, 1010 Northgate Dr., San Rafael, CA 94903. (415) 479-8800. Saturday 9AM to 4:20PM. $150.00.

2/28/04 — San Francisco, CA — Held at the Hyatt Regency SF Airport, 1333 Bayshore Hwy., Burlingame, CA 94010. (650) 347-1234. Saturday 9AM to 4:20PM. $150.00.

3/6/04 — North Los Angeles, CA — Held at the Hilton Woodland Hills, 6360 Canoga Ave., Woodland Hills, CA 91367. (818) 595-1000. Saturday 9AM to 4:20PM. $150.00.

3/20/04 — Phoenix, AZ — Embassy Suites, Phoenix-Biltmore, 2630 E. Camelback Rd., Phoenix, AZ 85016. (602) 955-3992. Saturday 9AM to 4:20PM. $150.00.

4/17/04 — San Antonio, TX — Held at the Abraham-Hicks Facility, 28550 Old Fredericksburg Rd., Fair Oaks, TX 78015. (830) 755-2299. Saturday 9AM to 4:20PM. $150.00.

4/24/04 — Atlanta, GA — Held at the Atlanta Marriott Century Center, 2000 Century Blvd. NE, Atlanta, GA 30345. (404) 325-0000. Saturday 9AM to 4:20PM. $150.00.

5/1/04 — Washington DC — Held at the Hilton Arlington, 950 N. Stafford St., Arlington, VA 22203. (703) 528-6000. Saturday 9AM to 4:20PM. $150.00.

5/3/04 — Philadelphia, PA — Held at the Philadelphia Marriott West, 111 Crawford Ave., West Conshohocken, PA 19428. (610) 941-5600. Monday 9AM to 4:20PM. $150.00.

2003-04 GENERAL WORKSHOP SCHEDULE

**Please reserve
in advance with our San Antonio office at (830) 755-2299.**

PREPAID RESERVATIONS ARE REQUIRED.

Following is general information for up-coming workshops. Specific location and other details will be provided when you make your reservation, or you may request this information at any time.

Time Format for following events:: 9AM to 4:15PM

10/25/03 . . . . . Saturday . . . . Asheville, NC	7/14/04 . . . . . . Wednesday . . . . Portland, OR
11/1/03 . . . . . . Saturday . . . . Dallas, TX	7/17/04 . . . . . . Saturday . . . . Ashland, OR
11/22/03 . . . . . Saturday . . . . San Antonio, TX	7/24/04 . . . . . . Saturday . . . . San Francisco, CA
12/6/03 . . . . . . Saturday . . . . Tampa, FL	7/25/04 . . . . . . Sunday . . . . San Rafael, CA
12/13/03 . . . . . Saturday . . . . Boca Raton, FL	7/31/04 . . . . . . Saturday . . . . West Los Angeles, CA
12/20/03 . . . . . Saturday . . . . Orlando, FL	8/1/04 . . . . Sunday . . . . . North Los Angeles, CA
1/24/04 . . . . . . Saturday . . . . San Antonio, TX	8/14/04 . . . . . . Saturday . . . . San Diego, CA
1/31/04 . . . . . . Saturday . . . . West Los Angeles, CA	8/28/04 . . . . . . Saturday . . . . Sedona, AZ
2/7/04 . . . . Saturday . . . . San Diego, CA	9/1/04 . . . . Wednesday . . . . Albuquerque, NM
2/21/04 . . . . . . Saturday . . . . San Rafael, CA	9/15/04 . . . . . . Wednesday . . . . Kansas City, KS
2/28/04 . . . . . . Saturday . . . . . . San Francisco, CA	9/18/04 . . . . . . Saturday . . . . Chicago, IL
3/6/04 . . . . Saturday . . . North Los Angeles, CA	9/22/04 . . . . . . Wednesday . . . . Cincinnati, OH
3/20/04 . . . . . . Saturday . . . . Phoenix, AZ	9/25/04 . . . . . . Saturday . . . . Detroit, MI
4/17/04 . . . . . . Saturday . . . . . . San Antonio, TX	9/29/04 . . . . . . Wednesday . . . . Syracuse, NY
4/24/04 . . . . . . Saturday . . . . Atlanta, GA	10/2/04 . . . . . . Saturday . . . . Boston, MA
5/1/04 . . . . Saturday . . . . Washington, DC	10/9/04 . . . . . . Saturday . . . . Tarrytown, NY
5/3/04 . . . . Monday . . . . Philadelphia, PA	10/13/04 . . . . . Wednesday . . . . . Philadelphia, PA
5/8/04 . . . . Saturday . . . . Tarrytown, NY	10/16/04 . . . . . Saturday . . . . Washington, DC
5/15/04 . . . . . . Saturday . . . . Boston, MA	10/23/04 . . . . . Saturday . . . . Asheville, NC
5/19/04 . . . . . . Wednesday . . . . Buffalo, NY	10/30/04 . . . . . Saturday . . . . Dallas, TX
5/22/04 . . . . . . Saturday . . . . Chicago, IL	11/20/04 . . . . . Saturday . . . . San Antonio, TX
6/5/04 . . . . Saturday . . . . San Antonio, TX	12/4/04 . . . . . . Saturday . . . . Boca Raton, FL
6/12/04 . . . . . . Saturday . . . . Boulder, CO	12/8/04 . . . . . . Wednesday . . . . Tampa, FL
6/19/04 . . . . . . Saturday . . . . Fort Collins, CO	12/11/04 . . . . . Saturday . . . . Orlando, FL
6/26/04 . . . . . . Saturday . . . . Seattle, WA	
7/3/04 through 7/10/04 . . . . Alaskan Cruise	

A Simple Choice: Which Thought Feels Best?

Vibrational Frequencies and Creations of Realities

Guest: I've heard for many years that we create our own reality, and I have always wondered, more specifically, how *do* we create our own reality?

Abraham: When you say, "We create our own reality" or "I create my own reality," the first thing you have to do is accept that "I" didn't just start with this body that was born back in whenever it was born. I am a very old being that has been projecting thought into this time/space reality long before my Spirit took part in this flesh. And so, I and others like me, have projected all of this.

GUEST: Okay. So what I'm understanding from you is that there are lots of different vibrational frequencies and groupings of frequencies, and the platform that is my current agreement has an average vibrational frequency. And it is out of that average frequency that my contrast occurs, and my desires come out of that. And all I need to do is use my Guidance System to sense the things that are basically of a higher vibration

> Long before my Spirit took part in this flesh, I have been projecting thought into this reality.

— things that make me feel better. And by controlling the focus of my attention on those things, then that pulls forth the Energy from my Inner Being that flows toward that and creates more of it...So, the main thing that I should be working on is my ability to focus and to maintain a focus?

Does Your Desire Feel Good?

Abraham: Here's the thing that we want you to hear: The contrast provides stuff to focus upon and gives you the variety that, naturally, without effort, gives birth to the desire within you. So that's just a natural consequence of coming into an environment that produces that.

So now, the desire is within you. It was born out of the lovely contrast, and now your work is, singularly, to align your Energy with this new-found desire, which means think about this subject that has been born within you — and feel good at the same time. That's the modulation process: *Think about your desire until it feels good. Think about it until it feels familiar. Think about it until feeling like this, feels like the*

C6

most normal thing in the world to you. And when you and your new desire are in alignment — then the manifestation occurs.

We often say to you: "Think about what you want and decide what you want; decide what you want." And the reason that you hear us hammering about that, so much, is because most people are running around making decisions about what they *don't* want. We are wanting you to let the contrast, of course, tell you what you don't want, but then always look for the nugget within it. We want you to feel the nugget, the prize, the wonderful uncovering. *The fresh new desire that is born is the reason that the entire Universe exists — and once the desire is born within you, then the Non-physical Energy will answer it.*

The saddest thing that exists in the human experience is when a being allows the contrast to let a desire be born, and then keeps himself, through old habits of thought, vibrationally out of sync with the new desire. Almost all of the philosophies that you have inherited, and that you teach to one another, on this planet about why things work the way they work, come from that "not understanding how I could possibly be deprived of the things that I want?" And yet it's such a simple thing, once you begin to understand the vibrational nuances, and once you begin to understand: *The reason*

> *Born of contrast, that new desire within you is the reason the entire Universe Exists.*

that I have feelings, is because of two things: I'm summoning the Non-physical Energy by virtue of my desire. And I'm allowing it, or not allowing it — by virtue of my thought or belief.

When we first began articulating through Esther, the words that we used were these: When your desire and your belief are the same — it is. And, in those early days, the words that Esther found to express what we are offering here, with many more words, said: When there is something that you want — you must believe it.

That's a hard thing for people to grasp, because you've been carrying some of these uncomfortable beliefs around for a long time. And we would like to help all of you let yourselves off the hook, because you can't buck Law of Attraction (That which is like unto itself is drawn). If you've been thinking this thought and thinking this thought and thinking this thought, that's the thought that's active in you now. And Law of Attraction is going to bring you more stuff that matches that thought all the time. And then you beat up on yourself. You say, "I shouldn't be thinking those thoughts," when, in truth, you can't stop thinking those thoughts, because your "radio signal" is programmed to those, and so Law of Attraction is bringing you more. That's the trouble that most people have with this business of "You create

Continued on page C27

C7

And Party Cat Too

Dear Abraham, Esther, Jerry, Tracy and everyone else and Party Cat, too: Thank you all for your efforts!!!

How about including Jerry's questions and comments more often on the tapes? I miss him. I always listen to the lead-in just to hear his voice!

I am enjoying *Tape of the Week...* The Seattle 7/4/99 tape was extra superb. If available, I'd like the tapes from the rest of the week-end.

Thank you, MM — CA

Alkie-Druggie Makes Changes

About six months ago I was introduced to an *Abraham-Hicks* tape by way of a therapy group. I am a recovering alkie-druggie, and most of my life I have shunned help, or any form of changing my narrow point of observation. At first, the message seemed too simple to be real! Maybe you were just another witch doctor handing out tickets for a movie that never shows!!! I began recognizing my skepticism as contrast, and found that it covered over more anger and fear. I found that I could use this to look at what I was wanting, or better yet, to discover through the knowing of what I didn't want, the way to start focusing and aligning thought and emotion. The more I've listened to the tapes, the more I hear the respect for individuation that Abraham expresses for those of us on this physical plane. Oh God! I'm starting to have such a powerful insight to my life and the way that I interact with the people, places and things. I now am certain that there is more than one way to change my life, and I have a profound sense of gratitude for all gifts that the universe bestows upon me. It's all a perfect match!

Thank You. RH — E-MAIL

Spiritual Soul Food

Please accept this as a heartfelt thank you for the spiritual food you have given me through your tapes and *Quarterly Journal.* I have not purchased materials from you but have been given tapes by friends.

As so many others have experienced, I have found your messages to be life-changing

and inspiring, and I am finally understanding how it is that I am getting what I am getting. I listen over and over to your tapes. I especially appreciate the *Law of Allowing.* It brings it all together for me. I bless you and look forward to reading and listening to more of your sharings.

NS — MT

A Unity Pioneer

Greetings from the Gold Coast of Queensland in Australia. The adventures I've had since coming home to live in Australia last June have been great! It has all unfolded that I'm pioneering a Unity Center here on the Gold Coast.

Just LOVE getting your *Quarterly Journal.* Literally keep them on my bedside table and just read and love and read and love. I have a certain amount of 'old fear tapes' that run, and the focusing on what I want gets difficult sometimes... so the newsletters are really important.

You and your work are always in my prayers. I don't know if you have been to Australia yet. Would love to see you here. I'm not "big enough" yet to be able to bring you out. I wish! However it is on my goal list.

Greeting and love for now,

GM — AUSTRALIA

His Life Has Transformed

The information from Abraham has transformed my life. Several years ago, at a point in my life that I had just said good-bye to a lover who had passed away, and when I didn't have the clarity I have now around dying, I said to a friend, "I just cannot find any joy." This friend was, and still is, a friend of Abraham. She took me for a walk on the beach, and then out to eat. We laughed together which felt so good. She then handed me the *Introduction to Abraham* tape. For the first time, I was hearing something, in it's totality, that rang true, and the information felt so good. I now appreciate the *Law of Attraction* every day. My life is full, I love my work, I have wonderful friends, and I look forward to every moment of living.

Again, thank you. MC — CA

Love ❥ Appreciation ❥ Love

Migranes To Mangoes

I enjoyed immensely the Spokane workshop on 7/7/99. My sister sent me your first book at Christmas 1998. Since that time, I've no longer had migraines. I have come to the understanding of how I had created them, along with everything else in my life. In seven short months my life has changed. I have been searching for understanding for 30 years. I wanted Abraham to come to Spokane and yet there was a fear of going, lack of money, not enough time (self-employed).... But I put my attention somewhere else and waited for the day, and it worked out just fine. Jerry is really funny!!! I even ate a mango the other day and enjoyed the deviousness of it (but not naked, although I did imagine it, ha ha).

DO — WA

Yes!!! I Did That!

I have been listening to your messages for about 6 months. My life has changed dramatically, and it is so much fun when I bring something into manifestation that I really wanted! I love it when I can say, "YES!!! I DID THAT!!!"

Love and blessings, KB — NE

Received Her Answer

I just returned from your workshop in Kansas City, and I want to thank you, and Abraham, for the information I received. This was my first seminar, and although I was not called upon to ask a question, I received an enormous answer to a question not even formulated until the afternoon of the first day of the seminar. I now know how to change my vibration regarding any issue. Abraham's vibrational "stick" was an excellent tool for me, and I'm sure it will be in the future.

Again, thank you very much. LB — KS

A Tape of The Day

Hello to all in Abraham-Hicks Land!

Since my recent move to Germany I switched from a Tape of a Month to a tape a week — and now I've decided that I need a tape a day! Tell Jerry to work on that!

Thanks sooooooooooo much!

Love and respect, LS — GERMANY

Unlocked Desire

I was one of the happy many at your recent Albany conference. It seemed to unlock my long held desire to teach and write! Every child's laugh, anyone's joyful excitement, no matter what the context, feels like a place for me to go to and springboard off their joy to even higher levels. I experience everything around me at that time as proceeding higher, and I now understand how uplifting others happens. This is a message of thanks to you, Jerry an Esther and to Abraham, and a message of "I am here... I have arrived!" I am in the world lining up my energies and desires to do what I came forth to do. Thanks for unlocking this door.

Gratefully yours, DD — NY

Joyful Knowing

How joyous that our Inner Beings led us to you two! To the answers we have yearned for — WHY and HOW, so completely and clearly, and we are joyful in our new knowing.

The *Quarterly Journals* were and are a pleasant surprise — plus, the *Introduction to Abraham* tape. Thank you for caring so much about the Truth.

Thanks a million, you marvelous folks, for you have warmed our hearts.

Love from, KL & DB — B.C. CANADA

A Whole New Level

I wanted to tell you how important this weekend workshop was for me and to thank you for the precious gift that you have bestowed. I left the workshop on this glorious day with an incredible lightness of being — a feeling that I still have at this present moment.

I am that much further along the path, and I want you to know what a significant role you have played. I have been listening to your tapes (really relistening) almost every morning for the past five months, I am now looking forward to receiving the *Tape of the Month* from you.

Actually experiencing the workshop brought me to a whole new level — especially in regard to understanding myself as a "leading edge creator" — there is a deep wellspring of energy there.

You are all such special people to me. I feel like I am part of your family.

Thanks again. RG — CA

The Book on Tape — Sara and Seth, Solomon's Fine Featherless Friends

Sara and Seth, Solomon's Fine Featherless Friends is now available as an unabridged book on tape. Containing three audio-cassettes, this album offers over four hours of inspiring, uplifting and adventurous listening.

Whether at the wheel of your vehicle or doing mundane chores or simply relaxing with closed eyes, you can now comfortably absorb the pleasure of this extraordinary magical relationship between Sara and her new friend of a feather, Seth... plus, her ethereal owl friend, Solomon, makes his welcome reappearance, adding his wise perspective to their/our learning experiences.

To order: S3SARAII — Sara *II*, The Book on Tape $30 plus S/H
(Order by phone 830 755-2299, or mail, fax, or on-line — page C24)

SPECIAL OFFER: For a limited time, when you order your Book on Tape album of *Sara II* for the regular price of $30 you may also receive a complimentary companion copy of the Book, *Sara and Seth, Solomon's Fine Featherless Friends*. Both included in your album price of $30 (plus S/H). Ask for "FREE SARA II" soft cover book when you order the Book on Tape. (See order form on page 43.)

Strong and Clear

An experience with *Sara and Seth, Solomon's Fine Featherless Friends* would benefit anyone, of any age, wanting to understand how they can change their lives, because, as Abraham says, the broader message is "wedged between the cracks" of this seemingly simple storyline. And the message is strong and clear: You are living what you are vibrating.

As Solomon says in the early part of the book, *Law of Attraction* (that which is like unto itself is drawn) is really behind everything that comes to you, or happens to you. And so, if you are a vibrational match to good things, then only good things can come to you... If you carefully observe the way you are feeling, and then you notice that what comes to you matches that feeling, you then begin to understand how *Law of Attraction* works. Then you understand that by changing the way you feel — you can change how things turn out."

Come, drink in Solomon's wisdom and feel the resonance inside as this wise bird rings your bells of self-discovery. The door to a joyous life experience awaits you.

reviewed by Cindy Saul (phenomeNEWS Magazine)
(and, again, I helped! Gerri Magee)

A Review of the Book Sara and Seth, Solomon's Fine Featherless Friends

...My family had read the first Sara book and were captivated by its wisdom and clarity. I knew we were in for a treat with this new story, "Sara and Seth", but I had no idea just how much of an impact it would have on all of us.

Seth is the new boy in Sara's mountain town... an "intense seeker" of answers to life's puzzling questions... Seth and Sara are drawn together (Law of Attraction) and embark on a wild, fun-filled, roller-coaster of a ride toward enlightenment and self-discovery.

Sara introduces Seth to Solomon (the wise old owl from the first Sara book) who, in turn, answers the questions that have plagued Seth... And as we are seeing Seth and Sara's growth and joy and understanding unfold under Solomon's tutelage, we the readers are also absorbing and processing the practical and spiritually uplifting information.

This book is truly a gift! It's like a gold-encrusted treasure chest laden with precious jewels. The only thing you have to do is pluck the pearls of wisdom that are strewn throughout the story and clutch them to your heart.

One such pearl for me was when Sara asked Solomon if he was mad or disappointed in her. The answer Solomon gave to her is one that I have committed to memory, for I know I will be using it with my own loved ones forever.

I had tears of happiness and gratitude streaming down my face when I finished this book, for it accomplished a *profoundly difficult* task — that of presenting the way the Universe (life) works in a *profoundly simple,* joyful and graceful way. *The sheer brilliance of this unassuming little book with its powerful message (of Well-being) will leave you breathless.* — by Denise Tarsitano in the "Rising Star Series."

Order: SARA II — Sara & Seth,
Solomon's Fine Featherless Friends!
$15 plus S/H — ISBN 0-9621219-7-5
ORDER BY PHONE (830) 755-2299 (OR BY MAIL, FAX OR ON-LINE — PAGE C24)

A Simple Choice: Which Thought Feels Best?

Law of Attraction is very powerful, and as you set your Tone, All-That-Is will respond to the vibration you have offered. You will always know by the way you feel how closely that resonates with who you are and what you have intended.

There is one flaw in human consciousness that if you could set it aside, would serve you enormously well: You keep thinking that there is a limit to the abundance. If you could understand that it is a never ending stream of abundance, and that there is no shortage whatsoever — you would soothe many basic issues that have been thwarting your motion forward.

You will never get it finished. It will continually expand to surprise and delight you. And no matter how it feels right now, you cannot get it wrong. Be aware of what unfolds in the days that immediately follow this, because you are in vibrational harmony with Source, and in the perfect place of allowing so many of the things that you've been asking for.

If your physical body wants healing, now is the time, because you are in the place to allow it. If more dollars are what you are seeking, they are rolling in. Expect it and let those opportunities come to you easily. If it is a relationship that you are wanting, you are closer and more on the brink of it than you have been, as you are in this moment in the place of allowing.

(Excerpted from Abraham-Hicks Workshop In Albuquerque, NM — 5/9/99)

G-3/21/99 — He's mentally hearing Christmas songs in April. Mr. Fixit is experiencing restless nights. Lawyer requests Abraham's perspective on litigation aspects. This nurse is smelling sweet Nonphysical beings. Considering some ecstatic aspects of sexual transmutation. Vibrational frequencies and creations of realities. Third set of teeth nubs aren't showing.

G-4/3/99 — Has reality turned your attention switch on? A good Energy vs. a bad Energy? She "wants" us all to stop wanting. Why different people gravitate to different teachings. To get to self-love quickly and easily? Body weight, as a work in progress. Religions, Jesus and Abraham of the Bible.

G-4/4/99 — Why that incomplete baby still feels secure. Wanting a partner who is "emotionally available". Reincarnation, continuity, individuality, Inner Being and time. Your vibration is where you last left it. Walk us through "weight loss without exercise". Why are we allowed our negative creations? Conflicting beliefs about weight loss systems?

G-4/11/99 — Source of the extraterrestrial river of paranoia. "Which feels better?" is the only question. Was his leper experience his favorite incarnation? No rights to impose war *or* peace. Choosing to allow children their own choices. Regarding time, eternity and the year 2000. Sara, Seth and Solomon's natural unconditional love.

G-4/24/99 — Desire, as the reason for this physical environment. Why do negatives attract her focused attention? Psychologist wants efforts to bring more dollars. Esther at airport, and "Hi! I'm Sierra!" Basis of Littleton High School teen shootings. Can anything be done to prevent shootings? Sudbury School, a positive picture to envision.

G-4/25/99 — See your perfection through a child's eyes. Envision prosperity for sake of your pleasure. Let's talk about keeping our manifestational score. Her vision doesn't include her current mate. Why come from peaceful Nonphysical to this? Cocky teenage son wants to drive car. Can we be uplifters and still evaluate?

G-5/9/99 — What is the best way to visualize $? She is gaming with the slot machine gamble. CARE, and helping others help themselves. Wants, instead, to awaken from dreams laughing. How can we love child killing children? Without protection, you're living a secure life. Can he allow his young son's anger?

G-5/15/99 — Is "All-That-Is" all there Is? Depression, as an indicator of powerful desire. Often awakens to a sense of terror. Should this activist turn his other cheek? Her lover ran around and then away. Singer is feeling a new sound of music. There is great love here for you!

G-5/22/99 — He's living happily with "full blown AIDS". How valid are the many diverse "Ologys"? Wants harmony between their many diverse animals. Sold business, now taking his first job. What is the possible value of mourning? Is this a wrong time for career change? Why does least wanted seem to come fastest?

G-5/29/99 — You will always have an unfulfilled desire. Molestation victim seems to attract more injustice. A crisis seen as a turning point. Here she is without a problem. She pinned selfish, noncooperative woodchuck with pitch fork. Not wanting to argue with her mate. When you feel better, they feel better.

ORDER: SPRING, 1999 CASSETTE ALBUM — $77.50 + S/H

Words For
A New Baby Girl
Excerpted from: G-8/2/98

GUEST: People here know that you have helped me create my beautiful baby girl who is the most joyful, sparkling thing I have ever seen in my life. Now if you could take it a step further and tell me everything you know about how to treat her at this stage in her life, or remind me of everything that I know.

ABRAHAM: Treat her as if she knows. Honor her ability to choose, and trust that, in time, she will learn how to choose. *Teach her, through the clarity of your example, which means, you cannot teach her connection unless you are connected. Do your dominant interacting with her when you are feeling your very best — and any time you don't feel that good, make yourself scarce from her.*

When she asks questions, applaud every one of them, and if you don't have the answer, still applaud her question. And let her know, early on, that the knowledge that she seeks, and the good that is natural to her, will come from all kinds of places — not only through you. *Encourage her independence from you, as quickly as you can, so that she can discover the thrill of creating on her own.*

Fill her with words of encouragement. If you find a moment of dissatisfaction with her, swallow it. Do not speak it. But let the desire that is born out of that, roll across your mind in the night. Develop it fully until you have visualized a full picture of what you know she is wanting, relative to any subject. And once you have come to feel familiar about that, then begin to express it to her.

When you speak to her, always speak what you feel. If you don't feel good, don't speak. If you are always speaking what you feel and you are only speaking when you feel good, what you are doing is always opening a vortex that connects with the Energy and always flooding it into the relationship that you are having.

If, as she grows, she finds something that displeases you, and you feel that it is your job to correct her, and you do, and you feel the negative emotion that is within you — know that, in this moment of teaching your child, your Inner Being is not there with you. Come to trust the way you feel, and express to your little one only in your times of connection. There is plenty of contrast out there for her. And in doing this, what you will teach her is what it is like to be with someone who is, for the most part, connected to Core Energy. You will give her an up close example of how well the Universe responds to someone who's in vibrational harmony with Source.

Protection is
Not Needed

It is not your job to protect her or guard her from anything, because there is nothing to be protected from unless you make it part of your consciousness. As she grows and begins to interact with others, there will be plenty who will be offering that information to her, and when that begins to occur, do not push against it. Do not feel that her connection is fragile. It isn't. She can get back to it easily. Impart to her: Her connection — that she is living fully now, and that you are learning or relearning and living much of the time — is not a fragile thing. You don't have to protect anyone from anything. Mostly, just get happy and stay there.

GUEST: People here know that you have helped me create my beautiful baby girl who is the most joyful, sparkling thing I have ever seen in my life. Now if you could take it a step further and tell me everything you know about how to treat her at this stage in her life, or remind me of everything that I know.

ABRAHAM: Treat her as if she knows. Honor her ability to choose, and trust that, in time, she will learn how to choose. *Teach her, through the clarity of your example, which means, you cannot teach her connection unless you are connected. Do your dominant interacting with her when you are feeling your very best — and any time you don't feel that good, make yourself scarce from her.*

When she asks questions, applaud every one of them, and if you don't have the answer, still applaud her question. And let her know, early on, that the knowledge that she seeks, and the good that is natural to her, will come from all kinds of places — not only through you. *Encourage her independence from you, as quickly as you can, so that she can discover the thrill of creating on her own.*

Fill her with words of encouragement. If you find a moment of dissatisfaction with her, swallow it. Do not speak it. But let the desire that is born out of that, roll across your mind in the night. Develop it fully until you have visualized a full picture of what you know she is wanting, relative to any subject. And once you have come to feel familiar about that, then begin to express it to her.

When you speak to her, always speak what you feel. If you don't feel good, don't speak. If you are always speaking what you feel and you are only speaking when you feel good, what you are doing is always opening a vortex that connects with the Energy and always flooding it into the relationship that you are having.

If, as she grows, she finds something that displeases you, and you feel that it is your job to correct her, and you do, and you feel the negative emotion that is within you — know that, in this moment of teaching your child, your Inner Being is not there with you. Come to trust the way you feel, and express to your little one only in your times of connection. There is plenty of contrast out there for her. And in doing this, what you will teach her is what it is like to be with someone who is, for the most part, connected to Core Energy. You will give her an up close example of how well the Universe responds to someone who's in vibrational harmony with Source.

Protection is Not Needed

It is not your job to protect her or guard her from anything, because there is nothing to be protected from unless you make it part of your consciousness. As she grows and begins to interact with others, there will be plenty who will be offering that information to her, and when that begins to occur, do not push against it. Do not feel that her connection is fragile. It isn't. She can get back to it easily. Impart to her: Her connection — that she is living fully now, and that you are learning or relearning and living much of the time — is not a fragile thing. You don't have to protect anyone from anything. Mostly, just get happy and stay there.

GUEST: I'm so busy because I'm working full time and I'm a single parent, and everything's going very nicely. I used to take three or four hours before I'd get those 17 seconds going. But when I did

The Book on Tape: Sara, and the Foreverness of Friends of a Feather

*S*ara and the Foreverness of Friends of a Feather is now available as an unabridged book on tape. Containing three audio-cassettes, this album offers over three hours of inspiring, uplifting and entertaining listening.

At the wheel of your vehicle or doing mundane chores or relaxing with closed eyes, you can now comfortably absorb the pleasure of this extraordinary magical relationship between young Sara and her ethereal, old, feathered owl friend, Solomon...

**Order: S3 SARA I — Sara I...The Book on Tape $30 plus S/H
(To order by phone 830 755-2299, or mail, fax or on-line — page C24)**

SPECIAL OFFER: For a limited time, when you order your Book on Tape album of *Sara I* for the regular price of $30, you may also receive a complimentary companion copy of the Book, *Sara and the Foreverness of Friends of a Feather.* Both are included in your album price of $30 (plus S/H). Ask for "FREE SARA I" soft cover book when you order the Book on Tape.

(Order form on page 43)

It Gets Better and Better

I finished the audio book of "Sara" and wanted you to know how GREAT it was. I especially like Jerry's voice and hope that he is considering reading the other books, too. I listen to your tapes every day as I'm walking my dogs, driving in my car, or working in my garden.

Thank you so very much for all the wonderful changes you have made possible in my life. I am looking forward to attending my first workshop in Detroit.

Thanks again, L.P. — @worldnet

Sara Receives Award of Excellence

"Dear Mr. & Mrs. Hicks:

It is my pleasure to inform you that *Sara, and the Foreverness of Friends of a Feather* has received a 1997 *Body Mind Spirit* Award of Excellence as one of 1996's outstanding books in print...

"Chosen from hundreds of excellent books in the areas of spirituality, natural healing, relationships and creativity...each book makes a valuable contribution to our self-knowledge and self-transformation...We commend the authors for these outstanding works..."

And Esther and I feel both appreciative of and blessed by the recognition of our beloved *Sara.*

A Review of the Book: Sara and the Foreverness of Friends of a Feather,

...My whole family read this book and we haven't been the same since. My husband, perhaps, was the most moved by it. He actually said that it had such a tremendous impact on him that he looks at life with new eyes. It's like being nearsighted your whole life and then finally getting glasses. Everything becomes crystal clear.

I cannot say enough good things about this life-transforming book. If there is only one book you ever buy, make sure it is this one. You won't regret it! (all ages) *by Denise Tarsitano in the "Rising Star Series.*

Excerpted from phenomeNEWS
"Mixed Reviews" 9/9/98

...*Sara and the Foreverness of Friends of a Feather* is a novel about a young girl, Sara, who learns about life through a wise owl named Solomon.

Readers will understand how they, too, can become the magnificent creators they were born to be and that all really is in divine order ... all really is well.

When Sara comes to this knowing, she asks her wise mentor, "Solomon, how ever will I ever explain this to anybody? How will I ever make them understand?" And Solomon speaks to all of us as he answers, "Sara that is not your work. It is enough, Sweet Girl, that you understand."

Sara is also available on audio cassette tapes. Jerry Hicks brings his show business background to a delightfully orchestrated version of the book as he breathes joy and vitality into each character. For children of all ages, from 5 to 105.

Sara and the Foreverness of Friends of a Feather is a wonderful gift to give yourself or anyone who wants a greater understanding of life. We highly recommend the book, and the Book on Tape — and all of the Abraham-Hicks material.
Reviewed by Cindy Saul (and I helped, too! — Gerri Magee)

And Abraham says, "This book will help you to remember that you are an eternal being... and it will help you to discover the everlasting bond that connects joyous loved ones to one another."

A Twelve Point Synopsis
of Abraham-Hicks' Teachings

1 *You Are a Physical Extension of That Which is Nonphysical.*
All-That-Is, or that which you call God, is not finished and waiting for you to catch up. You are the leading edge of thought, here seeking more: more of all that feels good to you, more of that which is fresh and gloriously uplifting. (You are, in essence, bringing heaven to earth.)

2 *You Are Here in This Body Because You Chose to Be Here.*
You chose the opportunity to experience this delicious contrast in time and space, and with great anticipation you came to co-create with other joy-seeking beings, to fine-tune the process of deliberate thought. (What, where, when and with whom you create are your choices, too.)

3 *The Basis of Your Life is Freedom; the Purpose of Your Life is Joy.*
You are free to choose to discover new avenues for your joy. In your joy you will grow, and in your joyous growth you will add to the growth experience of All-That-Is. (However, you are also free to choose bondage or pain.)

4 *You Are a Creator; You Create With Your Every Thought.*
By the Universal Law of Attraction, you are attracting the essence of whatever you are choosing to give your attention to — whether wanted or unwanted. And so, you often create by default. But you can know by how your emotion feels if what you are attracting (creating) is what you are wanting or if it is not what you are wanting. (Where is your attention focused?)

5 *Anything That You Can Imagine is Yours to Be or Do or Have.*
As you ask yourself why you want it, the essence of your desire is activated, and the Universe begins to bring it to you. The more intense your positive feelings, the faster it is coming to you. (It is as easy to create a castle as a button.)

6 *As You Are Choosing Your Thoughts, Your Emotions Are Guiding You.*
Your loving Inner Being offers guidance in the form of emotion. Entertain a wanted or unwanted thought, and you feel a wanted or unwanted emotion. Choose to change the thought and you have changed the emotion — and you have changed the creation. (Make more choices in every day.)

7 *The Universe Adores You for it Knows Your Broadest Intentions.*
You have chosen to come to earth with great intentions, and the Universe constantly guides you on your chosen path. When you are feeling good, you are, in that moment, allowing more of that which you have intended from your broader perspective. (You are Spirit Incarnate.)

8 *Relax into Your Natural Well-being. All is Well. (Really It Is!)*
The essence of all that you appreciate is constantly flowing into your reality. As you find more things to appreciate, your state of appreciation opens more avenues to more for which to feel appreciation. (As you think, you vibrate. As you vibrate, you attract.)

9 *You Are a Creator of Thoughtways on Your Unique Path of Joy.*
No one can limit where you can direct your thought. There are no limits to your joyous journeys to experience. On the path to your happiness you will discover all that you want to be or do or have. (Allowing others their experiences allows you yours.)

10 *Actions to Be Taken and Possessions to Be Exchanged Are By-products of Your Focus on Joy.*
On your deliberately joyous journey your actions will be inspired, your resources will be abundant, and you will know by the way you feel that you are fulfilling your reason for life. (Most have this one backwards, therefore most feel little joy in their actions or their possessions.)

11 *You May Appropriately Depart Your Body Without Illness or Pain.*
You need not attract illness or pain as an excuse to leave your body. Your natural state — coming, remaining or leaving — is that of health and Well-being. (You are free to choose otherwise.)

12 *You Can Not Die; You Are Everlasting Life.*
In grace, you may choose to relax and allow your gentle transition back into your Nonphysical state of pure, positive Energy. Your natural state is that of Foreverness. (Have fun with all of this! You can't get it wrong, and you'll never get it done.)

PS *It is not necessary for even one other person to understand the Laws of the Universe or the processes that we are offering here in order for you to have a wonderful, happy, productive Life Experience — for you are the attractor of your experience. Just you!*

Jerry & Esther Hicks — 11/95 (www.abraham-hicks.com)

SPECIAL SUBJECT TAPES — VOL I

FOCUSED IN OUR NOW, the only point in which we have the power to create — neither speculating into the future nor reminiscing into the historical past — ABRAHAM speaks, primarily, toward that practical information which we can personally learn to deliberately apply to our current experience and thereby gain beneficial results....From their broader perspective, unencumbered by your cultural beliefs, ABRAHAM reaches into a place, within you, of clear, primal acknowledgement, from which you will repeatedly hear that enthused inner "voice" reminding you, "I knew that!"

As you experience these Special Subject tapes, expect a fresh state of joyous becoming, for ABRAHAM'S words will stimulate you to a new beginning. Retain the beliefs that are of value to you, and learn to become unaffected by any acquired beliefs or influences that have been a hindrance. ABRAHAM guides us, first, to harmony with our Inner Being, and then all else falls into perfect alignment.

In order to build a foundation of an understanding of Abraham's teachings, begin with the tapes AB-1, *Free Introduction To Abraham,* through AB-6, Great Awakening and Blending, and then progress through the *Special Subject Tapes Series*—as per the order of your interest. Each tape addresses different levels of awareness, and as you repeatedly listen to them, as you are moving forward, you will continually be achieving new insights and experiences.

Order a single at $9.95, 3 or more at $7.75, or order 5 or more,
and receive a complimentary (while available) 12 space cassette album.
ORDER ANY COMPLETE SET OF 10 TAPES FOR ONLY $77.50 (PLUS S/H)
See page C24 for ordering information, or call (830) 755-2299.

AB-2 LAW OF ATTRACTION * — The most powerful Law in the universe. It affects every aspect of your daily life. A Law which is, whether you understand that it is or not. Specific processes are offered here to help you learn how to harness this Law — to get what you want.

AB-3 LAW OF DELIBERATE CREATION * — Discover the ecstasy of understanding universal Laws which are absolute — no matter what the circumstances. Without an understanding of this universal Law, it is as if you are playing in a game where the rules are not understood, so it is not only impossible to know if what you are doing is appropriate, but you do not know how to win the game. The rules of the game of life are clearly offered here.

SPECIAL SUBJECT TAPES — VOL I

AB-4 LAW OF ALLOWING * — Of all things that you will come to understand through this physical life experience, nothing is more important than to become an allower. In becoming an allower, you are free of the negativity that binds you. Learn the joyful difference between tolerating and allowing — and experience the blissful difference in every relationship you have.

AB-5 SEGMENT INTENDING — Our futures are individually paved by the steady stream of thoughts we set forth. We are literally creating our future life as we direct our thoughts of this moment into the future. Discover the magnificent power you hold in this moment — and learn how to use that power always to your advantage.

AB-6 GREAT AWAKENING, BLENDING — You have deliberately and excitedly chosen this time to be physical beings upon this planet, because you knew in advance that this would be the time when many — not all — physical beings would recognize the broadness and great value of their being. Follow this step-by-step process for awakening.

AB-7 RELATIONSHIPS, AGREEMENTS — We are all creators as we individually think and plan, but we are also often co-creators as we interact with others. Most relationships with others are far less than we want them to be. Find out why. Discover how to rejuvenate unhealthy relationships and attract new harmonious ones.

AB-8 BODILY CONDITIONS — Nothing is more important to us than the way we feel and look, and yet so many do not look or feel as they would like to. There is not a physical apparatus, no matter what the state of disrepair, that cannot have perfect health. Discover the powerful processes to bring your body to the state of being that pleases you.

AB-9 CHRIST CONSCIOUSNESS — While it can be satisfying to read and remember the teachings of the great ones who have gone before us, it is ever more joyous to discover the power of that knowledge within our own being. Learn the process to go within — as Christ encouraged — to experience the blissful oneness with Christ.

AB-10 ADDICTIONS — Habits, or compulsions, or addictions can range from annoying to destroying. Often, long after they are no longer wanted, they can bind and control your life. As you listen to this recording — you will for the first time understand exactly what the addiction is, and the simple process offered here will free you from it.

AB-11 JOYOUS SURVIVAL — While there are seemingly earth shattering events occurring in greater frequency upon your planet, you need not be affected by them. Discover how to create and control your experience in this seemingly unstable environment.

VARIOUS SERVICES AND PRODUCTS

MONTHLY SUBSCRIPTION CASSETTE OR CD PROGRAM

We select and edit from as many as 28 new Group Session Tapes that ABRAHAM produces in a month, a 74 minute recording of what we feel contains the most new, inspiring and thought provoking material. And we ship that 74 minute composite recording to the subscribers of the Monthly Subscription Program. *A gift that keeps on giving. Subscription fee: $12 per month for cassette and $15 per month for CD.*

• ...Enclosed, please find a check for another one-year subscription to the Monthly Tape Program. *...Every time I replay any one of those tapes, I realize that it has a whole new meaning for me... What a great way to start the day! My profound gratitude to you for sharing this wonderful way of life.* — New Jersey

• ...You do a wonderful job of editing the Monthly Tapes, because each tape seems to give the answer I need at the time. *Each month gets a little deeper and broader. It is so wonderful to have such guidance. You are what is needed on our planet now. Fondly* — Iowa

WEEKLY SUBSCRIPTION CASSETTE OR CD PROGRAM

For those who want to learn as much as they can "to be and have and do" as fast as they can and are not in the position to personally attend ABRAHAM'S ever evolving Workshops, we offer this Weekly Subscription Program: We choose, each week, what we consider to be the workshop with the most stimulating, practical, new ideas — or significant ideas presented from a new perspective — and we form a 74 minute composite recording and ship it to our subscribers. Four cassettes equal one month's billing. *Fill your spare moments with upliftment, flow and forward motion. Subscription fee: $10.25 per week for cassette and $12.50 per week for CD.*

• ...I'm so enjoying the Weekly Tape Program! Each new tape seems to get better and better! My life has been transformed in the three years that I have been listening to your tapes. *Every aspect of my life, every relationship I have, has been enriched and enhanced with the knowing of Abraham. I am eternally grateful for this information! With a full and joyful heart. Your friend* — Pennsylvania

GLUTTON SUBSCRIPTION PROGRAM

Be on a standing order to receive the uncut recordings of every Workshop. Subscription fee: $50 for each 4 cassette album. $60 for CD's (plus S&H)

WORKSHOPS & WEEKENDS

What do you want to more clearly understand?: Your state of becoming? Finances? Bodily conditions? Relationships? Business/Career? Metaphysicality? Your state of being/having/doing...? To participate in an open group "Questions and Answers" workshop with ABRAHAM, contact Abraham-Hicks Publications at (830) 755-2299 for dates, locations and to make your reservation.

• ...I was at your workshop in Chicago a few days ago, and I am still floating several feet above the earth. I had listened to the tapes and read some of the books but *being in the presence of Abraham and watching Esther's physical expression of this profound energy and passion has truly taken me to another level of being able to integrate this information more deeply and easily. Much love.* — Illinois

TO RESERVE OR SUBSCRIBE, CALL OUR OFFICE AT 830 755-2299

PRICE LIST

WORKSHOPS, WEEKENDS, SEMINARS — Details are posted in each Quarterly Journal on page 4. Call (830) 755-2299 for details of activities in your area.

STARTER SET — Cassettes: $35. CD's: $45. (See page 18) Album of five of Abraham's most powerful and popular recordings. (See ordering information on page 32.)

WEEKLY SUBSCRIPTION PROGRAM — Cassettes: $10.25 per week. CD's: $12.50 per week. One 74 minute composite of group sessions. Call or write to begin your Weekly Tape or CD Program. (See page 30)

MONTHLY SUBSCRIPTION PROGRAM — Cassettes: $12 per month. CD's: $15 per month. One 74 minute composite, each month, that offers the most new practical and inspirational material from Abraham, is selected and shipped to a group of subscribers. Call or write to begin your Monthly Tape or CD Program.

NEW! GLUTTON PROGRAM (4 TAPE WORKSHOP ALBUMS) — You may now order 4, 74 minute recordings (with flaws and flows) of complete workshops. Cassettes $50. CD's $60 (plus S & H). Call our office (830) 755-2299 for subscription details.

CASSETTE TAPES & CDs — $10 each. (CD's $15) Order 3 or more at $9 each (CD's 3 or more $12) — or order 5 or more (in same "Set", "Volume" or "Season") and they will be shipped to you in a complimentary, (a limited offer) convenient 12 space cassette album. Abraham's "AB Series" – Special Subjects 74 minutes, and their "G-Series" 74 minute group session composites are all priced the same: $90 for the album sets of 10, (CD's $117) $10 for singles (CD's $15) or $9 each (CD's $14) when ordering 3 or more. (Plus shipping and handling.)

BOOKS — $15 each. Pay $12 each when ordering 3 or more. (Plus shipping and handling) Study groups, teachers or dealers, call for volume discount when ordering 9 or more books. (See page 40-45)

3 TAPE ALBUMS — $30 each (plus S/H). Currently these include our Sara Books on tape and Abraham's Greatest Hits albums. (See page 38, 42, 48, 52-55)

DAILY PLANNING CALENDAR/STUDY GROUP WORKBOOK — A 768 page planning, implementing and manifesting calendar to utilize for your personal creation, or use it as a Course Workbook for a 12 month Group Study. $25 (plus S/H). *Check it out; satisfaction guaranteed.* (See page 36)

VIDEO CASSETTES — For prices and details of offerings see page 28 & 60 of our complimentary Catalog (Quarterly Journal, Volume 24) which includes all materials created from 1988 to 2002. (See pages 24-27 & 49-51)

TRANSCRIPTIONS — Many 90 minute Abraham recordings have been transcribed and are now available for $10 each (plus S/H). On line, $5.

QUARTERLY JOURNAL — "The Quarterly Journal of *The Science of Deliberate Creation*" — Published 4 times a year by Jerry and Esther Hicks. (Current issues are complimentary while in stock. Back issues can be ordered for the minimum packaging and delivery fee of $5 each while supplies last.) Other countries pay postage only.

CATALOG — Complimentary full color 112 page compendium of the first decade of Abraham-Hicks teachings, from 1988 to 2000. Over 600 cassettes, books and videos.

FREE INTRODUCTION TO ABRAHAM-HICKS — This 74 minute recording is an ideal way to introduce the concepts to someone you love. The basics are all here! Specify tape or CD format and include $5 for minimum shipping and handling. (See page 35)

WEB SITE — Visit our up-dated Web Site: www.abraham-hicks.com. Free downloads of *Free Introduction to Abraham*, 74 minutes, or a sample of *A New Adventure* Music CD.

ORDER FORM

ORDER BY TELEPHONE: (830)755-2299 or FAX (830)755-4179

Order on-line at www.abraham-hicks.com (a secure transaction)

Mail To:Abraham-Hicks Publications — P.O. Box 690070, San Antonio, TX 78269

NAME _____

ADDRESS_____ APT NO: _____

CITY _____ STATE _____ ZIP_____

TELE: (HOME) _____ (WORK) _____ (FAX) _____

REFERRED BY:_____

SHIP TO: (If different from above name or address) Is this a gift? _____

RECIPIENT'S NAME _____

SHIPPING ADDRESS_____ APT NO: _____

CITY _____ STATE _____ ZIP_____

SPECIAL INSTRUCTIONS:_____

(TO SHIP BY UPS, WE NEED YOUR STREET OR RR NUMBER — NOT A P.O. BOX)

STOCK#	QUAN	ITEM DESCRIPTION	PRICE
AB-1/CD-1		Tape or CD: Free Introduction To Abraham (min. S/H only)	$5.00
ST-CD		Starter Set: Abraham's Basics in CD Format @ $45	
ST-TP		Starter Set: Abraham's Basics in Cassette Format @ $35	
ABVONE		Cassette Album: 10 Special Subjects @ $90	
ABVTWO		Cassette Album: 10 Special Subjects @ $90	
ABCN		Daily Planning Calendar/Workbook @ $25	
G SERIES		Album: 10 Group Series Tapes @ $90 or CD's @ $117 (specify which)	
ANBI		Book: A New Beginning I @ $15	
ANBII		Book: A New Beginning II @ $15	
SARA 1		Book: Sara & the Foreverness of Friends of a Feather @$15	
SARA 2		Book: Sara & Seth, Solomon's Fine Featherless Friends @ $15	
SARA 3		Book: Sara 3, A Talking Owl is Worth a Thousand Words @ $15	
S3SARAI		Book on Tape: Sara 1 in 3-Tape Album @ $30	
S3SARAII		Book on Tape: Sara 2 in 3-Tape Album @ $30	
S3SARAIII		Book on Tape: Sara 3 in 3-Tape Album @ $30	
		Abraham's Greatest Hits in 3-Tape Albums @$30 (specify which)	
		Write in desired Individual Special Subject Tapes or CD's, Group Series Tapes or CD's, Videos, etc.	

Call (830) 755-2299 to reserve your space at any of our Workshops. Call or write if you have questions
regarding subscribing to a tape or CD program.

ORDER FORM, CONTINUED

Please enter totals from your order on previous page	ADD TOTAL OF ITEMS
	ADD SHIPPING AND HANDLING (SEE CHART)
	TEXAS RESIDENTS, ADD 8.25% SALES TAX
	TOTAL AMOUNT ENCLOSED

☐ Personal Check: (Payable to Abraham-Hicks Publications — US Funds only)
☐ MasterCard ☐ VISA ☐ American Express ☐ Discover

Card # _____   Exp Date _____

Cardholder's Signature _____

SARA 1 (12/03)

Print Name_____

HOW TO ORDER

ORDER BY MAIL, PHONE, FAX OR INTERNET

BY TELEPHONE — (830) 755-2299

BY FAX — (830) 755-4179

BY INTERNET — (Secure transaction.) www.abraham-hicks.com.

WE SHIP UPS, FEDEX OR US POSTAL SERVICE

We usually ship within two working days of your order and UPS usually is best for larger orders. Please specify any preferences.

INTERNATIONAL ORDERS

We ship USPS (unless requested otherwise). Call us for current shipping rates outside of the continental USA.

PLACING ORDERS

- Please print or type information
- List stock number (i.e. AB-1) and its price.
- Pay with check (US funds only), money order, or MasterCard, Visa, American Express or Discover credit card.
- A replacement order form will be enclosed with each shipment.

DEFECTIVE OR DAMAGED TAPES OR BOOKS

Call, write or email telling us the title series date and problem and we will replace, or refund cost of the item. (We no longer refund shipping costs.)

We are most appreciative of the many suppliers of services and materials who make it possible for Abraham's words to reach you so efficiently. As costs of doing business are increased, or decreased (taxes, inflation, etc.) to any of our suppliers and passed on to us, we, in turn, through our varied business transactions, reflect those changes back into the international economy.

ADD THESE SHIPPING COSTS		
U.S.A.	**CANADA**	**ALL OTHER**
Up to $29.99 .... $6.00	.... $7.20	.... CALL
$30 to $49.99 .... $9.00	.... $12.20	.... CALL
$50 to $99.99 .... $12.00	.... $14.50	.... CALL
Over $100 .... $16.00	.... $19.60	.... CALL

THANK YOU!

Our thanks to you for your role in this joyous co-creation. Your thoughts as we interact, your pondering, questioning, recognizing, knowing and wanting... add to our forward motion and to the fulfillment of our purpose.

We intend to allow ABRAHAM'S *words of perspective, positive guidance and stimulation of thought, to go as far and as fast as they are wanted. At the same time, we intend to continue our abundant, positive, mental, material and spiritual experience — and we do appreciate your contribution of "thoughts, words and deeds."*

Do you have a friend who would enjoy our Quarterly Journal?

Name (Please print) _____

Address _____

City/State/Zip _____

Your name _____

* EDUCATORS—TEACHERS—STUDENTS *

Are you involved in education and interested in an uplifting perspective? We can mail to you (at no cost) a copy of Daniel Greenberg's *Free At Last*, highlights of the first 20 years of the remarkable Sudbury Valley School experience. We have a few remaining copies (not for sale) just let us know if you would like one and we'll get it off to you as soon as it is practical.

This book will make your heart sing!

(We ship this book only to the one who is requesting it.)

OUR UNCONDITIONAL
GUARANTEE OF SATISFACTION

We are aware that due to technical or personal idiosyncrasies you may receive a damaged or defective or unwanted item from us — but we will replace it or refund your money (whichever you prefer) just as soon as you call or write and give us the details. Unless we request it, please don't bother with shipping the item back to us. Just toss it away, or pass it on. We want you to be completely satisfied with our products and our service.

Jerry & Esther

Packaging & delivery (S/H) costs are no longer refundable.

your own reality." Try as you will, you can't buck that current, you see.

Dormant Beliefs Don't Affect You

We don't want you to try to buck that current. We want you to start setting a Tone that is more in alignment with the current that is really already you. *You can be chuck full up to the brim wtih beliefs that do not serve you well — and not one of them will affect you unless it is activated. And when it is activated, you'll have a feeling response to it.*

When a belief that is not in harmony with your Source Energy is activated, you'll get that funny feeling in your stomach. And as you get that funny feeling in your stomach, what it is telling you is: This thought in this moment does not match who you are and what you are wanting. And so, you have a simple choice. You can go with it, you can try to beat it to death, you can get people together, you can try to isolate it, you can add to it and get it bigger and bigger, or you can, as Jesus said, turn the other cheek, and allow that vibration to become inactive again, while you are tuning your vibration to that which feels better.

If It Feels Good, Choose It

And so, you see, it's all about choices. Which feels better? Does it feel better to be connected to my Source, or not? Connected would feel better! Clarity or confusion, which feels better? Vitality or a tired body, which feels better? Abundance or poverty, which feels better? Connection or resistance...?

And so, it isn't complicated, but we have to do such a sales job to convince you dear beings that it is right for you to seek that which feels good. Somehow you've come to believe that if it feels good, you should be feeling guilty about it. If it feels good, there must be something wrong with it. And we say, however did that become such a big part of your mass consciousness, when there is not a shred of evidence that supports that anywhere in the Universe?!

Everything's out there pulsing. So here's someone experiencing a terrible experience. And I see it. And I don't want it. I don't want it for them, and I don't want it for me. But as I address it, my "switch" is on. So I'm not only adding to it for them, I'm adding to it for me. Now most humans would say, "Well, Esther, do not turn away from this and put your head in the sand." And Abraham would say, Esther, turn away from this — and achieve vibrational harmony with something else.

If Esther sees some horrible thing and she says, "No, no, I want not that, what I want is...," and out of this abhorrent thing a desire is born, and Esther is wise enough to turn her attention now only to the desire, and find vibrational harmony with the desire — now that situation has benefited All-That-Is, because something very powerful and very good has come out of it.

But if Esther does like many people do, and gets stuck in what she sees here, so she suffers, in despair, and adds to the negative, or even if she takes the next step where she says, "Oh I don't want this, I don't want it to touch me," and looks away, but then feels guilty

Continued on page C44

C27

SPECIAL SUBJECTS TAPES — VOL II

...I AM A MEDICAL DOCTOR and have not, before, run across material that has this much potential to create health...Have enjoyed Abraham's books and tapes beyond any expectations I had when my mother originally sent them. I would like to subscribe to your "Weekly Tape Program". Thank You.
CHRISTIANE NORTHRUP, MD.— ME

AB-12 PIVOTING & POSITIVE ASPECTS * — If I am the "Creator of my own experience", why don't I have more of what I want? Fostered by an action oriented world, most of you do not understand your true nature of attraction, thus the confusion in why you are getting what you are getting. These processes of pivoting and the book of positive aspects will assist you in the self-discovery of what is important to you, and will put you in the strong, clear place of well-being, so that you can allow what you want into your experience.

AB-13 SEXUALITY — Love, sensuality and the perfect sexual experience — pleasure vs. shame. This misunderstood issue lies at the heart of more disruption in the lives of physical beings than any other issue. Discover the true nature of your being, and release yourself from the negative turmoil that surrounds the subject of sexuality.

AB-14 DEATH — Aging, deterioration and the perfect death experience — choices vs. chances. The gathering of years is a natural experience. However, deterioration of your physical body is neither natural nor necessary. Be healthy and productive and active and happy until the very day of your chosen re-emergence into the Nonphysical.

AB-15 DOLLARS — Abundance, in perfect flow — gaining the freedom that dollars can bring vs. losing your freedom while gaining your dollars. As there is an abundance of the air you breathe, so there is an abundance of the dollars you seek. Listen and learn how to relax and breathe in the fresh air of freedom offered to you through the abundant flow of dollars.

AB-16 HEALTH, WEIGHT & MIND — The perfect states of weight, health and mind — how can I get there and stay there? Diet plans abound and research continues and yet the number of those unsuccessful at maintenance of satisfactory bodily and mental conditions increases. Understand how your body functions and why you are as you are — and then begin your swift and steady progress toward that which you desire.

AB-17 MATING — The perfect mate: getting, being, evoking one — Attracting vs. attacking. While it is your natural endeavor to co-create with others, there are few who have discovered the bliss of magnificent relationships. Find out how you can experience the joy of a perfect union.

SPECIAL SUBJECT TAPES — VOL II

AB-18 PARENTING — Perfect harmony between my children and me — and me and my parents. Harmonizing vs. traumatizing. While often disconnected from parents, either by death or by distance, your parent/child relationships often have great influence in your experience with your children or with your current life experience. Learn how to perceive what has been in a way that is beneficial to your now rather than destructive. Let that which you have lived be of value.

AB-19 CAREER — The perfect career. What, where and when is it — and what can I do about it now? With so many exterior standards or rules regarding the appropriateness of your behavior or choices — in most cases more confusion than clarity abounds. Use this process to discover and attract that which is perfect for you. Stop the futile backwards approach — and begin creating from the inside out.

AB-20 SELF APPRECIATION — If I am so "Perfect as I am" — then why don't I feel better about me than I do? Selfishness vs. selflessness. Your awareness of your perfection was intact as you emerged into this physical body, but it was soon sabotaged by the critical, comparing, judgmental world that surrounded you. Rediscover your true sense of value and well-being and perfection.

AB-21 INNER GUIDANCE — Tell me more about my Inner Voice? Because you have thought in terms of being dead or alive, you forget that you are, simultaneously, physically focused while another part of you remains focused from Nonphysical perspective. Once remembering that the inner you exists, you may begin to listen to what your Inner Voice is offering. Here is the process for re-establishing that important conscious connection.

FREE 90 MINUTE INTRODUCTION TO ABRAHAM TAPE

A stimulating overview of Abraham's basic message: How to consciously harmonize and interact with your pure, positive Inner Being...How to realize who you are and why you have chosen to be physical in this time...How to joyously and deliberately utilize the Laws of the Universe to Attract all that you are wanting to be or have or do....Also, Jerry & Esther summarize the process of their introduction to Abraham. This cassette is a comfortable means to share Abraham with those who seek a new way of realizing a successful life experience. (Order AB-1. * Include $5.00 Minimum S/H)

...Since receiving ABRAHAM'S *Free Introductory Tape,* I've listened to it 3 or 4 times. It is concise and very recreatable both in my life and in my work as a consultant...*I wanted to thank you for so much value in this one small tape. I am impressed and moved...Enclosed is my first "real" order.—Texas*

Quarterly Quotes from Abraham-Hicks

Within the seed of your desire is everything necessary for it to blossom to fulfillment. And Law of Attraction is the engine that does the work. Your work is just to give it a fertile growing place in order to expand.

Albuquerque, NM — 5/9/99

The entire Universe is set up to produce wanting within you! You cannot squelch wanting. You are born wanters. Wanting is a good thing. Write that down in big letters: *WANTING IS A VERY GOOD THING!*

Tarrytown, NY — 5/15/99

Desire summons Life Force. If we must continue to be alive, we must continue to have new desire. *You are not willing to let yourself outrageously want because when you outrageously want something that you haven't found a way of getting, it is too uncomfortable, and the risk feels too great.* We're wanting you to hear that there is no risk at all! Fantasize and watch what happens.

Chicago, IL — 4/24/99

Your action has nothing to do with your abundance! Your abundance is a response to your vibration. Of course, your belief is part of your vibration. So if you believe that action is part of what brings your abundance, then you've got to unravel that.

Chicago, IL — 4/24/99

What "moving thought forward" is, is about being a nucleus that attracts different components of thought so that when they actualize around you — it is different than it has ever been before!

"As I stand in my focused, human, leading-edge experience, and I choose this combination of thoughts and feelings, I am offering a signal that has never been offered before. And so, the Universe must uniquely yield to me, which causes me to offer a vibration that maybe someone somewhere else is matching. If they are, they will certainly come into my experience for the time that we are matching it." That is the way you affect the world.

Most think in terms of thought affecting the world: You think about transmitting outward: "I'm going to affect the world from my outgoing signal." That isn't the way it works. You affect the world by achieving the vibration that brings the signals to you. You create a nucleus that Universe has to respond around. That is how you are the creator.

Albuquerque, NM — 5/9/99

You were "predetermined" to have a joyful, expansive experience, and the way in which you will do that is all up to you. All other choices are for your physical format. *Everything is still in the process of being created. There is no creation that has reached its completion.*

Albany, NY — 5/22/99

There are no choices that are really a detour that will take you far from where you're wanting to be — because your Inner Being is always guiding you to the next, and the next, and the next. So don't be concerned that you may make a fatal choice, because there aren't any of those. You are always finding your balance. It's a never ending process.

Albany, NY — 5/22/99

The premise that so many people come from is that good isn't natural; good must be demanded or manipulated or orchestrated. And we say, *good IS natural! It must be asked for, and it must be expected — but Good is the only Stream that flows.*

Tarrytown, NY — 5/15/99

If you knew everything was really all right, and that it always has a happy ending, then you would not feel trepidacious about your future. *Everything is really so very all right! If you could believe and trust that, then, immediately everything would automatically and instantly become all right.*

Silver Springs, MD — 4/11/99

You never get it done, and you cannot get it wrong. Life is supposed to be fun: you are creator, you are a focusing mechanism, and you are here in an environment that is very conducive to that. *When you get hold of an idea,*

Quarterly Quotes from Abraham-Hicks

play it out for the pleasure in it. If you are doing it for any other reason, then you are not connecting to your Source Energy.

Silver Springs, MD — 4/11/99

*Y*ou will always, almost always, most of you, choose negative emotion over no emotion. Because emotion indicates desire. It's exciting!

Silver Springs, MD — 4/11/99

*Y*ou are always living a reflection of whatever you are outputting. And so, if you get into a little pocket where a lot of people are being rude, it's probably because you are being rude — or because you have been aware of people being rude. *Nothing ever happens to you that is not part of your vibration!*

Chicago, IL — 4/25/99

*I*t is your rules that make unlawful beings. You would get along better if you would just trust each other to treat each other appropriately, but you don't. So you keep making laws — until you make criminals of everyone.

Chicago, IL — 4/25/99

*I*f we had a child, or anyone, and we caught them doing something inappropriate, we would not amplify it with our words. We would identify what it is we do not want, and then out of it would come the rocket of desire of what we do want, and then we would just visualize, visualize, visualize, until we find peace within our vision. When you make someone and their action the heart of a vision that you've spent time on — your relationship improves, your experience is better, and they receive the benefit of the experience.

But if you catch them, and see them, and worry about it, and put mechanisms in place to prevent it, now you have not only amplified it, you have now made a commitment that is hooking you both into that, until usually it gets big enough that you break apart, and then you attract others to fulfill that role.

Chicago, IL — 4/25/99

*A*s you begin to state what you do want, rather than clamoring about what you don't want, you come into your own power. *When you come into your own power, you feel better. And when you feel better — those who love you also feel better.*

San Antonio, TX — 5/29/99

*T*he best thing you could do for anyone that you love, is be happy! And the very worst thing that you could do for anyone that you love, is be unhappy, and then ask them to to try to change it, when there is nothing that anybody else can do that will make you happy.

If it is your dominant intent to hold yourself in vibrational harmony with who you really are, you could never offer any action that would cause anybody else to be unhappy.

Chicago, IL — 4/25/99

*I*s harmony one note that everybody is singing? Or is it a whole lot of notes that are in vibrational harmony with each other?

When you give your attention to anything, the Universe responds to it. When two of you are giving your attention to it, and there is no contradiction, it is a powerful vortex. That's why a gathering such as this can achieve a great deal, as you come together in greater and greater harmony and take thought beyond that which it has been before.

Chicago, IL — 4/25/99

*M*ilk every moment for all the pleasure you can get from it. When you say, "It is my dominant intent to look for things that feel good, today. No matter where I'm going, no matter what I'm doing, no matter who I'm doing it with, it is my dominant intent to look for what I'm wanting to see, to look for things that feel good," and the more you develop the habit of that kind of vibration — the more the Universe understands that that's who you are! And so, the more you have access only to those kinds of things!

Albuquerque, NM — 5/9/99

WORDS OF WISDOM FROM THE BROADER PERSPECTIVE

In the minute you try to limit anybody about anything, you are defying the Laws of the Universe. It cannot be done. We are an expanding Universe. It's not your job to corral any of it or to control any of it or to curtail any of it or to inhibit any of it or to dispose of any of it or to drop a bomb on any of it... It is not your work to deal with those things you do not want. Your work is to let those things you do not want produce within you the clarity of what you do want and then find vibrational harmony with that. Then, like a magnet, your world becomes a world that only has access to those things you have determined are the things you want to be. You are in no way inhibiting or preventing anyone else from living what they are living, but you are controlling and creating your own reality.

PRESENTING A POWERFUL 365 DAY COURSE IN SPIRITUAL PRACTICALITY

Habits are usually created slowly. And since a major aspect of the value to you of using this material will be the changing — often slowly — from unwanted habits of thought to habits of thought that are more appropriate to your current conscious desires — *the most common use of this calendar will be as a joyous 365 day journey into a new world of leading edge thought and experience.*

Begin experiencing the power of this calendar at any time. You don't have to wait until the first of next year. However, in order to get into time sequence with the calendar — it is best to start at a month's beginning. Let the first day of your first month be day one (page three) of this calendar.

After over 30 years of studying, teaching and enjoying the art of personal fulfillment, I have long understood the power of clarifying and writing out my decisions in appointment books, journals, organizers, etc. But as the years passed, I became aware that at the most joyous and highly productive seg-

ments of my life — I simply carried, daily, a fresh, updated sheet of paper in my pocket. This works!

The first sides of the pages are compilations from the best of the Abraham teachings. The second sides of the pages are designed to accommodate your daily list of things to do. *But as the course progresses, you will discover that the pages will be offering processes and techniques to fit the advancing stages of your progression within these materials.*

Your only power to create your life is in this moment, and the Abraham-Hicks Planning Calendar is designed to focus the purest of your intentions to your todays, the time in which you have your creative power.

In our estimation, this Abraham-Hicks Planning Calendar/Workbook is the most effective tool available for the practical application of "The Science of Deliberate Creation." Utilize it to create and to teach others to create, the perfect (by your ever changing standards) adventure in living.

> *"If you want to change what you are living,*
> *you only have to change the balance of your thought." — Abraham*

THE SCIENCE OF DELIBERATE CREATION

Abraham-Hicks Daily Planning Calendar
and Study Group Workbook

A 365 DAY COURSE IN SPIRITUAL PRACTICALITY

- The material in this calendar/workbook has been specifically intended as an experiential guide to comfortably change your balance of habits of thought to that which will enrich every aspect of your experience

- Begin in any month. The pages are left to be dated by you.

- This is a study to do, not a study to simply peruse. It is a study to have fun with in every way that you can imagine.

- The pages are the size of two $100 bills, side-by-side. Tear out a page a day. They are portable. Fold them into your wallet or checkbook, or simply carry them in a pocket. On one side you will find life enriching reminders of some things you may have forgotten and on the other side you can write intentions, ideas, names, numbers. Post them on your mirror, refrigerator, the sun visor of your car...

- Carry a seven day segment or a vacation segment with you when you are away from home — and then file them for future reference.

— Let the Magic Begin —

SELF HELP FROM YOUR TOTAL SELF

ORDER: PLANNING CALENDAR (768 PAGES) $25 USA

BOOK: A NEW BEGINNING I

THIS EXTRAORDINARY BOOK is powerfully offered by a group of teachers who call themselves Abraham. They express clearly and simply the laws of the universe, explaining in detail how we can deliberately flow with these laws for the joyful creation of whatever we desire. Abraham describes this as the time of awakening, explaining that each of us chose, with very deliberate intent, this specific time of great change to participate in this physical experience. This is an empowering, life-changing book that will assist you in seeing your personal life experience as you have never seen it before.

...The breakthrough book that started a worldwide interest in Abraham. Now in it's eigth printing, *A New Beginning I* explains in simple terms the eye-opening fundamentals of living a life of health, wealth and happiness. — Texas

COMMENTS:

• Thank you for a delightful book—*A NEW BEGINNING I*—a life changing book...a joyous do-it-yourself book...I have always known this was an "inside job", but I've not known, before, how to communicate well with the "inside." — Germany

• We are thrilled with the data. Everyone we have sent the book to thinks it is the best book they have ever read. — California

• The feedback I've gotten on the many *ABRAHAM* books that I have distributed has been phenomenal and it has come from all over the world. — California

• The first edition of *A NEW BEGINNING I* sold out because readers love the practical ideas of Abraham. In the tradition of Jane Roberts, this refreshing new book reveals a unique blend of new-age thought with the Western desire for "more." An inspiring self-help classic that gets results.

Softcover. $15.00. 218 pages. ISBN 0-9621219-3-2.
(To order, see page C24, or call 830 755-2299).

BOOK: A NEW BEGINNING II

THIS IS AN UPLIFTING BOOK that strikes a chord with the very core of your being. Written by Abraham to assist you in understanding the absolute connection between your physical self and your inner self, Abraham puts this physical life experience into perspective as they explain and define who we really are and why we have come forth as physical beings. This book is filled with processes and examples to assist you in making a deliberate conscious connection with your own Inner Being, that you might find the awesome satisfaction with this physical life experience that can only come once this connection is made.

...Now in it's sixth printing, *A New Beginning II* contains uplifting new material from Abraham including *Law of Attraction, Law of Allowing,* and the effective use of your *Guidance System.* Includes questions and answers from live workshops, affirmations, and powerful processes for increasing your ability to intentionally create WHATEVER you want. Incredible! A must read! — Texas

COMMENTS:

*   Your book, *A NEW BEGINNING II,* has been my constant companion, now marked and circled on page after page...So—UP with the "Fairies of the Universe" and beautiful music and laughter! — France

*   ..I hugged the book; I couldn't put it down for two days....You should see my metaphysical library—and of every book I have, this is the clearest! — Germany

*   Thank you so much for the book—it is the best yet. I like to open it at random and see what the good word is for the day. — California

*   Like the book before it, *A NEW BEGINNING II* is clear, practical, inspiring and empowering with more focus on how to realign with your Inner Being. The bottom line for Abraham-Hicks is to choose to feel good in every moment. From that base of joy you will naturally and easily create what you want for yourself and the world.

Softcover. $15.00. 258 pages. ISBN 0-9621219-1-6
(To order, see page C24, or call 830 755-2299)

ABRAHAM'S GREATEST HITS

"...I received the 3-tape set expressed in San Francisco, and with great delight I listened to the first tape a few days ago and am still vibrating in great appreciation. I have just now been with the 2nd tape, and it is profoundly resonating within me in a kind of paradoxical giggle...as I feel like a kid eating an ice-cream cone with sprinkles on it and simultaneously experiencing the profound tranquility and excitement of an adult who organically knows everything *is* all right as I continue to have the appetite for more. I am deeply appreciative. — R.E. — CA

THE SCIENCE OF DELIBERATE CREATION
ABRAHAM-HICKS PUBLICATIONS

San Francisco, CA — 2/20 & 2/21/99
(4 hrs. 30 minutes of Classic Abraham)

TAPE ONE
- You live in a flexible self-created reality.
- Are there better choices than world peace?
- Regarding: "I'm only human; I'm not perfect."
- How much tennis would be too materialistic?
- To maintain my Tone while observing unwanted?
- Interact with as many people as you can.
- Tell us about the merry old souls?

TAPE TWO
- AIDS carrying survivor considers rejoining dating pool.
- Birth control pills, do they affect natural selection?
- Abraham's perspective of celibacy, orgasms, etc.
- Brief series of Abraham's past one-liners.
- She really, really, really resents men.
- Do fathers always have to be right?
- To understand relationship between sex and violence?

TAPE THREE
- Is child's weight perpetuating classmate's teasing?
- Teach children through clarity of your example.
- How much action to do or not?
- Total financial freedom for her family?
- Where is the place here for compassion?
- What if mate dies and I'm left alone?
- Focus Wheels, Meditation and a screaming kid.

Order S3SF — $30.00 plus S/H

ABRAHAM'S GREATEST HITS

This is the special *Chicago, 3 Tape Album* that has evoked so much praise from our *Weekly Tape Program* subscribers. This was a Workshop that generated much too much new and fun material for us to edit down to anything less than this 4 and 1/2 hours of Classic Abraham.

THE SCIENCE OF DELIBERATE CREATION
ABRAHAM-HICKS PUBLICATIONS

Chicago, IL — 10/31 & 11/1/98
(4 hrs. 30 minutes of Classic Abraham)

TAPE ONE
- Learn to find familiarity with pure desire.
- Is that another Declarative Statement you're making?
- Wants Soul Mate, but enjoys current variety.
- How does OOB experience relate to one's Soul?
- Am I, indeed, on right path to wellness?
- Can she love her unlovable teen son?
- Would true friends kick a happy cat?

TAPE TWO
- Their feelings about you affect only them.
- Every belief was once a conscious thought.
- Your current reality was once a pretense.
- Is not grief appropriate at funerals?
- This is how eternalness is eternally eternal.
- How can they get out of "work hell"?
- About her seven year old psychic son?

TAPE THREE
- How does Abraham select the Workshop questioner?
- The next logical step to experiencing a "Frank".
- Did time stop when he fell from the bridge?
- Balancing children's educational structure with freedom.
- Is a "genetic" pain a genuine pain?
- Let's have more clarification on "Vibrations".
- Nurse wants to understand purpose of husband's death.

Order S3CH — $30.00 plus S/H

QUESTIONS AND ANSWERS

Cocky Teenage Son Wants to Drive Car

GUEST: I have a 16-year old son who needs to drive with his mom for 25 hours before he can get his license. I can't decide which is more horrifying, sitting with him and doing it, or thinking of him driving with one of his friends.

ABRAHAM: His friends, who are not petrified with fear, would be far better for him. Which feels better, to envision him making a mistake and killing himself, or to envision him a sharp and clear and connected and effective driver? Which feels better, to see him as a bumbling idiot who can't learn? Or to see him as a bright young man who does well at many things? Which feels better, to see him as insecure, or to see him as confident?

GUEST: Oh, he's confident, that's the problem. If he were a bumbling idiot, I would be okay. It's the cocky "I-can-do-anything" that makes me crazy.

ABRAHAM: Well, you don't need to worry about him. His self-confidence is a sign of connection. And in his connection, he'll be inspired. And you may not know this, but more of your Inner Beings are doing the driving than you are, and that's why it works out so well. And so, if you spend a lot of time drumming into his head all of the things that could go wrong, you will be more conducive to his Inner Being not being allowed with him when he drives. If you understand that all is well with him, and encourage him — then things will go better.

As youngsters have negative experiences that sometimes cause accidents or even take their lives, you take that data, and then you assume that it has something to do with your child, when it doesn't have anything to do with your child.

You do not know what the vibrational state of being was of those kids that died in traffic accidents. But you assume that whatever it was, is what your son's doing, and you want him to stop. And we are here to promise you that his confidence and that are a mismatch. If he is confident, and eager, and alive — those are matches to Well-being. You are wanting to imbue your son with your confidence in his ability. Otherwise, what you say is, "I don't trust you."

GUEST: It's very hard for me to be trusting with my son, 'cause there's been a lot of evidence to the contrary.

ABRAHAM: That evidence came from mistrust, which came from something else. As you don't trust, he responds to that, then you catch him and the consequences are so uncomfortable that he learns greater deception. And as he learns greater deception, then you don't trust him all the more, which means he gets even more deceptive...because you will never ever, no matter how hard you try — squelch his desire, that comes forth from within, to be independent. What we are saying to you is: *It is your rules that make unlawful beings. You would all get along a lot better if you would just trust each other to treat each other appropriately, but you don't. So you keep making laws — until you make criminals of everyone.*

QUESTIONS AND ANSWERS

The Greatest Gift To Give To A Child

Your children came forth pure and eager and knowing that all is well, to try to remind those who have come before them of something that they have forgotten. And so, that's why the generation gap will always be there. These bright young beings come forth feeling invincible, and their parents, who are not feeling so invincible, spend most of their life, teaching them to feel less and less invincible. And we say, how backwards is that? *You're wanting your children to be empowered. Self-empowered. That is the greatest gift that a parent can give to a child!*

The most effective parent is the one that gives birth and gets out of the way! Always there, lovingly, to answer anything that is asked, certainly, but not with that domineering, "Well I've lived, and I've had lots of experiences, and this and this and this has happened, and this is how it is, and the sooner you come to understand how it is, the better you'll get along in this world..." And your child says, "That's how it is for you, but that's not how it is for me." And you say, "Oh, well, you haven't had the experience that I have had." And your child is saying, "But you just have your own narrow, warped perspective, Mother. And your perspective doesn't have anything to do with me!"

You want your child to have a glorious experience, so just remember that for your child to live a glorious experience, he must be connected to Source Energy. So anything that you do that encourages that connection, is helping. Anything that you do that discourages it — is not.

So if we had a child, or anyone, and we caught them doing something inappropriate, we would not amplify it with our words. We would take the hit, and we would identify what it is we do not want, and then out of it would come the rocket of desire of what we do want, and then we would just visualize, visualize, visualize, until we find peace within our vision. And when you have taken someone and their action as the heart of a vision that you've spent time on — your relationship improves, your experience is better, and they receive the benefit of the experience.

But if you catch them, and see them, and worry about it, and think about it, and put mechanisms in place to prevent it, now what's happening is you have not only amplified it, you have now made a commitment that is hooking you into that, so that the two of you are now hooked together in this thing that you do not want, until usually it gets big enough that you break apart. And then you individually go off with your same vibration. And then you attract others to fulfill that role that you've set up together.

You're here to amplify in each other an opportunity to eternally find your connection. So then we come around again: Which feels better, to see him as self-sufficient and thriving? Or to see him as diminished in his ability and struggling? Which feels better, to see him as an effective, safe driver, or to see him as a reckless, careless driver? Which feels better, to see him connected to Non-physical Energy...?

Excerpted from Abraham-Hicks Workshop Chicago, IL — G-4/25/99

C39

G-SERIES TAPES WINTER, 1998
DOES THIS FEEL LIKE THE NEXT LOGICAL STEP?

G-10/18/98 — Is a joyous life, purpose enough for you? Expand your time by leveraging your Energy. What does she attract to her babies? Next logical step to a life partner. Wants to speak for her Spiritual Guide. About "year 2000 fourth dimensional" concern. Is "being wowed" the next logical step?

G-11/14/98 — Anything you give your attention to, expands. When hurt feelings are most familiar vibration. What clothes would a natural being wear? There is enough Well-being for everyone. You have your own direct connection. Does her deceased grandfather participate on stage? When persecutors die, are they then persecuted?

G-1/10/99 — Can a truly happy person get poison ivy? When her legs move correctly: "Good job!" Abnormal blood pressure led to weight-loss motivation. Different physical healing strokes for different folks. Disturbed by spending $40,000 on walk-in closet. YK2000 millennium fear threatens her Well-being. Pottery maker feels limited by his selfness.

G-1/16/99 — She believed her purpose was to right wrongs. Wealthy and healthy but fearing death and poverty. When Eastern masters deny their natural desires? A mother's greatest gift to her children. When choosing "dangerous" adventure over boredom. Can we change thoughts in our dreams? Payment received in Energy flow of project.

G-1/17/99 — Having it to want is what matters most. How can one's lack of health not matter? Mother wants a baby that doesn't scream. Wants trim body without giving up anything. What makes a woman most beautiful? Psychologist concerned about adopting child. A magnificent closing statement of Well-being.

G-1/30/99 — Her fears become a self-fulfilling prophecy. Negative declarative statements aren't serving you well. Words for infant daughter's christening celebration. Spending 17 seconds focused upon new work. To participate as an ideal citizen. Should he seek balance as job nears? He's considering inventing an energy detection gadget.

G-1/31/99 — Why does he get opposite of wanted? Keeping the essence of our identity forever. Gynecologist questions the limits of self-healing. Rage over Hitler's injustice serves you not. Does abortion deny a soul an opportunity? To help her sister get more sleep? Can this doctor dissolve her bodily dichotomy?

G-2/7/99 — Can one release clinical depression without drugs? Do the dolphins change to please you? To not match her children's uncomfortable vibrations? Dessert, and your slender, energetic, beautiful body. Asking for ways to fan our desires. Their tithing envelope is getting quite full. Questioning pre-birth agreements to physical restrictions.Å

G-2/27/99 — Have you a desire for perpetual youth? Her influence regarding suicidal brother-in-law? Wants enough dollars to give much away. Dad has been diagnosed with "terminal illness". Professional is overwhelmed by career details. Unsatisfactory grades on her doctoral program. Independent pre-teen has discovered political talk radio.

G-3/13/99 — Y2K headlines, and the value of greed. About rumored secret government health conspiracies? Resolving his fundamental conflict re: "good and evil"? Allow and uplift his family of ministers? Wants to preserve diverse regional worldwide cultures. Whining little child is disobeying family rules. Lessons learned through President Clinton's perjury trials?

G-8/22/98 — All comes in response to your vibrational offering. You pay a great price for your empathy. Practitioner wants to honorably integrate Abraham's materials. You can't impeach your leader into connection. Wants the low-down on "Mercury in retrograde"? Abraham's philosophy regarding cussing, swearing children. Who is responsible for the "victim's plight?

G-9/5/98 — How can we impact Nonphysical from Physical? Your fresh, powerful present rockets of desire. Evaluating others from your current ethical biases. Contrast ain't necessarily conflict or trauma. Now, she does want to bear a baby. Law of Attraction and its influence on births. Is this co-dependency or is it co-creativity?

G-9/6/98 — Receiving conscious communication from Nonphysical. When tragic deaths become next logical step. That "vengeful, angry, punishing God" never existed. About the dynamics of tithing? Yipping, clattering, eternally linking, neighbor's dog. Yipping, clattering, eternally linking, "horrible" tenants. Wife's religious perspective doesn't embrace his.

G-9/13/98 — Wants constant conscious connection with Inner Being. She is 38 and single and (bleeped). Caught up in children's rage and cynicism. How about her last 3 significant relationships? Tell me about "being present in my now"? Fears she has denied physical entry to spirits. She has a recurring hair loss problem.

G-9/27/98 — Creational X,Y,Zs and the variables of time. What they are addicted to, is feeling good. His lucrative, 4 days a week, profession feels unfree. Attorney loves, and dislikes, aspects of her profession. Are Pintos n'Cheese stuck in her chakras? "At your age", what do you expect? Wants to synthesize his Rockets of Desire.

G-10/11/98 — Focus Wheels, Place Mats, Creation Boxes and Dollars. Lotteries, and the exchange of human energy. A review of Abraham's Prosperity Game Process. Student wants un-work-related dollars. 17 Second Process to having enough time. Launching of children's program is bogging down. Do we choose when and how we die?

G-10/13/98 — All creation is on the leading edge. Are we, at some point, homogenized beings? She always falls asleep after she eats. Can our prayers override another's intentions? To deal with her ornamental bushwackers. Focus Wheeling 50 pounds weight loss worries friends. Questioning the nature of Nonphysical time.

G-10/15/98 — You did not learn to smell, you smelled. When seeking the cause of her discomfort. Can this prosecutor protect victims from victimizers? Which came first: chicken or egg? Can we communicate with plants and animals? Teen is "flipping off" her angry mother. Why does this cultural pity party exist?

G-10/17/98 — Inspired, or motivated, to her new job? What being fully connected feels like. The real purpose of Esther's tree house. Is resistance natural to our physical form? No "joy in heaven" from pain on earth. Clarification of "We are all one." A new perspective of "Families of Consciousness".

G-11/1/98, III — How does Abraham select the Workshop questioner? The next logical step to experiencing a "Frank". Did time stop when he fell from the bridge? Balancing children's educational structure with freedom. Is a "genetic" pain a genuine pain? Let's have more clarification on "Vibrations". Nurse wants to understand purpose of husband's death.

G-SERIES TAPES SUMMER, 1998
MONITORING YOUR VIBRATIONAL METER

G-6/14/98 — Abraham's tenth year with Unity of Fort Collins. She wants to do like Esther does. Faced with a "peanut butter" project at work. She loves their personal experience with Abraham. Allowing, accepting or resisting "Senior Citizenship". To remove his attention from his diabetes. Let's talk about conditional living.

G-6/20/98 — Let's talk about your infinite Vibrational Meter. Why didn't her furiousness create worse results? How can we shift our protective stance? Rebuilding your body weight belief system. When "terrible" things happen to innocent babies? Gerontologist seeks an "ageless" life until death. Abraham's Prosperity Process and robust "agelessness".

G-6/21/98 — Are the pendulum's answers valid regarding others? Chiropractor questions Non-physical aspects of healing. What if your rules required bigamy? He's got alien bones on his mind. She plummets through extremes of career contrast. Staying in a state of perpetual creative motion. Should parent protect child from a dis-empowering teacher?

G-6/27/98 — You have this Vibrational Meter within you. Why does Abraham neither laugh nor cry? "Can't worry and love children at same time?" Loves to serve, but money evokes her fear. When alien thoughts create alien thought forms. Climb aboard a butterfly, and use your imagination. "Live in the world but not of it"?

G-7/11/98 — How much allowance to give to children? She gained 40 pounds in three years. Why to begin playing Abraham's Prosperity Game. Abraham of the Jews, Christians and Muslims. To be less sensitive to influence of others? To communicate relief to her ailing grandmother. Where was Abraham before the earth evolved?

G-7/25/98 — Aerial view of your Rockets of Desire. Tears, at births, weddings and funerals? Seeking inspired careers in alternative traditional healing. His patent has been infringed; now what? Is there a cosmic form of birth control? When one's unwanted lover keeps hanging on? Son resists thanking grandfather for unwanted.

G-8/1/98 — What does Abraham mean by "the Universe"? Why he buys high and sells low. Rockets of Desire, connecting to your Well-being. Retirement, as not necessarily in one's best interest. Wanting to believe that "All is Well." She remembers Grandmother's teeth in a glass. Would Jesus do it differently this time?

G-8/2/98 — What would Christ say to us today? Caring for this beautiful new baby girl? Why is she collecting "inappropriate jerks". Best to ask for specifics, or in general? Magical appearance of a second career decision. How about this attorney's unforgiving nature? My body, my PMS, my unwanted cramps?

G-8/15/98 — Why you'll never not feel negative emotion. A rocket of desire to weigh less. How does Non-physical Energy enter physical body? Get me and my Thunderbird out of this. Inner Being isn't speaking rude words to you. Deceased mother smiles lovingly in his dreams. From regal riches to doldrums, now what?

G-8/16/98 — To be an empowering, allowing "Fairy Godmother". Bucky's body's buried; where is his beingness? Can a thought thought think it's thinking? Is performing "hard work", right or wrong? Wants to strangle her day-job co-workers. Does dirt work as well as "manna"? Looking for love in all the wrong places.

G-SERIES TAPES SPRING, 1998
FRESHNESS OF YOUR ETERNAL NOW

G-3/4/98 — After the Place Mat, then do what? Will vibration of joy bring only good? Which of these thoughts feels best? Focus Wheeling creations of a slender body. Addressing the concept of wasted natural resources. But, what if everyone wasted resources? My abundance does not deprive anyone else.

G-4/4/98 — Learn to consciously feel your Creative Tension. Can he harness and utilize his Energy? Are you driven by inspiration or by motivation? To enjoy the process of becoming organized. Focus Wheeling preparing her taxes in joy. Is "poormouthing" kin out prospering prosperity student? How many dollars could you spend tomorrow?

G-4/5/98 — Dream contact with essence of dead friend. Medicate child or beat him down? Balancing "I'm not safe" with "All is well". Resolving the enigma of her migraine headache. Concerning depending on an undependable relationship. Positive language question about "Wanting to try". Wants quantum leap in other aspects of life.

G-4/11/98 — Insight into the Non-physical part of you. Chances of achieving a lawsuit victory? Jerry and Esther's gate crashing landscaper. What is life like without physical bodies? Seeking the easiest way to appreciate self. Why Abraham doesn't see that "all's not well." The thing that will serve you best.

G-4/14/98 — Feel the Freshness of Your Eternal Now. The healing power of your connected thought. Does your illness allow another's wellness? Will group think world into peace? Can Inner Being's desire conflict with ours? Questioning the source of communicative Thought Forms. If it feels good, it is good.

G-4/25/98 — Make more eager decisions in every day. Was rusty skyscraper in Jerry and Esther's destiny? How decision resolves relationship discomfort. Can she have time and dollars too? Focusing one's thoughts on pleasing prosperity binge. Can new environment alleviate nurse's health issue? Significance of recovering alcoholic's recurring dreams?

G-5/10/98 — Why is her new secure money evoking fear? Can we learn channeling from a book? Understanding specific versus general attracting scenario. When the children ask about suicide. Act much less and imagine much more. Abraham discusses her child's "learning disabilities" label.

G-5/16/98 — How about that June 18th asteroid crash? Can dream career replace her realistic job? Considering a focus on diverse religious icons. Tears of overjoyment or of overwhelment? What isn't Abraham yet telling us? Her suicidal, school loathing, teacher hating child. Wants an overall view of his direction.

G-5/18/98 — Discover the freshness of your powerful now. Magical points of intersection of our thoughts. Focus Wheeling his career hampering fears. Conflicting emotions regarding their joyous divorce. What pre-birth choices are made from Non-physical? Seeking a dividing line between Source and selves. Prosperity game for practicing the flow of Energy.

G-5/23/98 — When the manifestation spark goes "pop". Can a child be spoiled by well-being? She specifically desires a specific lover. Wanting a slender body in two months. Scripting an appropriate body of 120 years. My body will always match my intentions. She feels resistant to her teacher's criticism.

Continued from page C27

because she's not helping — no good comes from any of that. Then she has just started one of those other vibrations, so all kinds of bad things start showing up in her experience. And then, on her tombstone, it says, "See, I told you this is how it was."

Esther is always reaching for the best possible feelings that she can find prior to one of these gatherings, because she wants to be as connected as she can to Source Energy before you begin summoning Abraham through her. And she said to Jerry, this morning, "What's one of the best feelings that you can ever remember from one of these gatherings?" She was reaching for a feeling. And Jerry said "Are you asking for a room or a face or a question?" Esther said, "I'm reaching for the feeling." And Jerry said, "Well, I always love the feeling at the end of the session, when everyone is feeling fulfilled and satisfied and connected and glad and empowered and secure, and knowing who they are." And Esther said, "Yeah, that's what I meant, that's what I meant." She's reaching for the feeling, the feeling of empowerment. *There isn't anything in the world that feels*

better to a teacher than to empower another.

In This Moment, Which Thought Feels Better?

Let's say that someone made you feel a little insecure. And out of that feeling of insecurity is born, in this moment, a stronger-than-usual desire to feel empowered and know who you are. *Use whatever means you need to, but just reach for the best feeling. How did it feel? What's the best feeling?* And so, here's this new desire pulsing, this fresh new nugget. Oh, it's alive and well, summoning Life Force through you, right here in the now. So here you're feeling it, right now. This fresh, new desire. And then, you just try to remember ever having felt like you now want to feel. And just by reaching for that, just by saying, "Have I ever felt like that?.." right away, those things will become be active again in your memory of when you felt like that. And you'll say, "I remember this, and I remember this, and I remember this... and you'll cross the 17-second mark and the 34-second mark and the 51-second mark focused on that which feels good, and you'll stand here in your powerful now, having activated every powerful moment that you've ever lived. And here it is, an apex, a

> As you choose thoughts that feel better on day one, on day two, you'll have access to a whole different set of choices.
> And on day three, there'll be available to you, a whole different set of choices — because each day you will have re-established your Vibrational Tone to your pure, positive Source Energy.

Continued on page C45

Continued from page C44

vortex, right here and now. This is what you've achieved, all out of some little slight that someone offered you. Oh, what a gift that was!

The Eternal Evolution of Spirit

Just go through your day-to-day experience, let your exposure happen as it will, because Law of Attraction says that it must, and when and if you get an emotional response — whether it is positive or negative — stop in the middle of that feeling, and acknowledge whether it's connecting you to Source or not. If it is connecting you to Source, go with it. Milk it for all it's worth. If it isn't connecting you to Source, but doing the opposite, then take your pivot: "I know what I don't want. What is it that I do want?"

Let the desire be born, and then try to find the feeling place of that. Try to remember something else like that. Come back into your power. And then stand on that new platform where you will now have access to things in your environment that a moment ago, you didn't have access to. This is the eternal evolution of the spirit that is pulsing within you.

Jerry and Esther checked into a hotel, and the person at the front desk was in a terrible mood. And as Esther stood there, she couldn't help but take responsibility for her rendezvous point with it. And that even irritated her more. It's bad enough that somebody's being rude, but to accept your responsibility in meeting up with them...

And so, Esther thought about it and realized that it was sort of where she'd last left her vibration about that hotel, and so it was logical. And as she was talking to us about it, she was still wanting to say, "But Abraham, don't you think that maybe it would be beneficial for the hotel to know that they have a really rude person behind the desk?" And we said, well, but which feels better, to pursue that thought, or to choose another thought that feels better? And Esther said, "Well, yeah, yeah, yeah. But Abraham, don't you think that under these conditions, shouldn't somebody call somebody? Shouldn't something be done about this?"

The business person in Esther, says, "Well, if my employees are mistreating people, I would like to know about it." And we say, no, you wouldn't. You're better off not knowing about it. In other words, let Law of Attraction shake it all down. You don't have to be the monitor of that sort of thing.

You have one question: Which feels better? Which feels better, this thought or this thought? Sometimes that seems like such a big thing to choose from, because there are infinite thoughts, but there are not infinite thoughts in this moment. In this moment, your environment is so perfectly established. In this moment, there are only a certain number of thoughts for you to consider. Not too many for you to choose.

As you start, on day one, deliberately choosing the thought that feels better — on day two, you will have access to a whole different set of choices than you would have if you had not made those choices on day one. And on day three, there will be a whole different set of choices now available to you — because each day you will have established your Vibrational Tone to your pure, positive Source Energy.

C45

Until in thirty days of playing with this, you can be a living, breathing, eating, light being.

Being Deliberate Does Take Practice

But it takes some practice to say, which feels better? Which feels better, this thought of my mother, or this thought of my mother? "But Abraham, you don't understand. This is who my mother is, mostly." That wasn't the question. Which feels better, this thought or this thought? "But Abraham, you don't understand..." That wasn't the question. Which feels better, is the only question—that's the only question that your Guidance System is asking. Which feels better, this thought or this thought?

Which feels better, to praise or to criticize? "Oh, but you don't understand, there's nothing to praise and there's lots to criticize." That's not our question. Which feels better? Which feels better? "But Abraham, you don't understand. You didn't see what happened." No, we didn't. We're not vibrating there with you. But our question to you is, which feels better, which feels better? "But, but, but, but Abraham, you need to be here where we are so that you understand what we're trying to tell you." Which feels better? — is the only thing that your Guidance System is asking you.

So which feels better, to pronounce to the world or to myself, I'm not free? Or to pronounce to the world, I can make more decisions?

*Nobody can get inside your head and make you think. Sometimes it feels like it, because they're clamoring in your face so loud with whatever they're saying. But you have the abil-*ity, *if it is your desire, to feel good. You have the ability to withdraw from whatever thought is bothering you, get off to yourself, and reclaim your connection to Source Energy. And that is the freedom that you are looking for.*

You have the ability to look here where there is not resistance. Jesus said, to turn the other cheek, and that's exactly what he was talking about. Resist not evil. Turn the other cheek — and achieve vibrational harmony with that which feels better.

All of you have access to Source Energy! It is always within you, always radiating through you. Sometimes you are providing a shadow that doesn't let it shine, more than others, and sometimes you are letting it shine fully. But the more you are letting the fullness of who you are radiate through you, the better you feel about everything — and the more you are contributing to the whole of things. However, in any case, you cannot get it wrong!

This article was excerpted from
Workshop Tapes:
Phoenix, AZ — 3/21/99 and
Silver Springs, MD—4/11/99

ABOUT THE AUTHORS

Excited about the clarity and practicality of the translated word from ABRAHAM, Jerry and Esther Hicks began, in 1986, disclosing their ABRAHAM experience to a handful of close business associates. Then, recognizing the practical results being received by those persons who began plying ABRAHAM with meaningful personal questions regarding their finances, bodily conditions, and relationships...the Hickses made a conscious decision to allow ABRAHAM'S teachings to become available to an ever widening circle of

Esther & Jerry Hicks

seekers. And that circle continues to expand — even as you read this page.

Jerry and Esther have now published more than 300 *Abraham-Hicks* books, cassettes and videos, and have been presenting open group interactive workshops in about 40 cities a year to those who gather to participate in this progressive stream of thought.

Although worldwide attention has been given by leading edge thinkers to this *Science of Deliberate Creation* who, in turn, incorporate many of ABRAHAM'S concepts into their books, lectures, sermons, screenplays, scripts...the primary spread of this material has been from person to person — as individuals begin to discover the value of these materials in their practical, personal experience.

ABRAHAM, a group of obviously evolved teachers, speak their broader Non-physical perspective through the physical apparatus of Esther. *Speaking to our level of comprehension, from their present moment to our now, through a series of loving, allowing, brilliant yet comprehensively simple, recordings in print and in sound — they guide us to a clear connection with our Inner Being — they guide us to self-upliftment from our total self.*

COMMENTS FROM READERS & LISTENERS:

...It's hard to believe that life could be so simple and so joyous and that it could take me so many years to find out how to do it...So, thank you, so much, for making an already good life even better! (With lots of good feelings) SC — PA

...I've been a "searcher," "seeker," "sharer" since I was a teen. My middle name was purported to be "Why?" The information from Abraham is so down-to-earth, useful, compelling, exciting, sensible, practical, empowering, clear, usable. I'm a marvelous deliberate creator now. Thanks for putting the "fun" back into physical life. JS — AZ

...Am so delighted to be reading your books, listening to your tapes, attending your seminars and talking to each of you on the phone. I am so happy and getting happier and clearer every day. My life has been leading to this point, and it feels like the icing on the cake. I know everything will just get better, although it's hard to know how. What a powerful gift you've given us — the recognition of our ability to create the life we want, and the tools to carry out the plan. Thank you for sharing. — CA